Benjamin

Franklin

Young Printer

Illustrated by Ray Quigley

Benjamin Franklin

Young Printer

by Augusta Stevenson

Aladdin Paperbacks

Aladdin Paperbacks
An imprint of Simon & Schuster
Children's Publishing Division
1230 Avenue of the Americas
New York, NY 10020

First Aladdin Paperbacks edition, 1986
Manufactured in the United States of America

20   19   18
Library of Congress Cataloging-in-Publication Data

Stevenson, Augusta.
    Benjamin Franklin, young printer.

    Reprint of the ed.: Indianapolis : Bobbs-Merrill,
c1983.
    Published 1941 under title: Ben Franklin, printer's
boy.
    Summary: A biography of the young Philadelphia printer
who grew up to become a world-renowned author, diplomat,
scientist, and inventor, and one of the founding
fathers of the United States.
    1. Franklin, Benjamin, 1706–1790—Childhood and
youth—Juvenile literature.   2. Statesmen—United
States—Biography—Juvenile literature.   3. Printers—
United States—Biography—Juvenile literature.
[1. Franklin, Benjamin, 1706–1790.   2. Statesmen.
3. Printers]   I. Quigley, Ray, ill.   II. Title.
E302.6.F8S885   1986   973.3'092'4 [B] [92]   86-10786
ISBN 0-02-041920-1

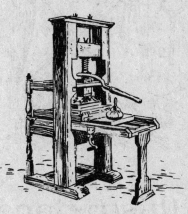

Dedicated to my brothers,
Benjamin and Frank,
who were named for
Benjamin Franklin

Illustrations

Full pages

Numerous smaller illustrations

Contents

Books by Augusta Stevenson

Benjamin Franklin

Young Printer

At the Sign of the Blue Ball

A LONG TIME AGO, away up in New England in the little city of Boston there was a certain blue ball. It was about the size of a cocoanut, and it hung above the front door of a certain little house. On this blue ball was a name—

Josiah Franklin

That was all, but it was enough. Everyone in Boston knew that the blue ball was the sign Josiah Franklin used for his candle-and-soap shop in Union Street.

They knew that he lived in this little house, too, as most tradesmen did in those days.

They knew that the shop was in the front room facing the street, and that the Franklin family lived in the big room just back of it.

They knew there were only two rooms on the ground floor, so this back room had to be kitchen, dining room, and living room, all in one.

But no one knew how many Franklins would be at home at any one time. Not even Mr. Franklin or Mrs. Franklin knew that. They could count on six of their children just now.

At any time, however, any one of their four married daughters might come for a visit and bring her children.

Their son Josiah, a sailor, might return. They were always expecting him. Now it was about time for son James to come home from his printer's job in England.

No matter how many were at home, there was always room in that big kitchen around the big fireplace and at the long, narrow table.

At the head of this table on a certain winter night in 1714, sat Father Josiah Franklin. He had just asked the Lord's blessing on the food about to be eaten.

At the other end sat Mother Abiah Franklin, a pretty woman with a pretty smile.

On the table in front of her was a huge white porcelain tureen with a porcelain ladle. It was really a soup tureen, but tonight it was heaped high with yellow mush. In fact almost every night, the year round, it was used for mush.

The table was lighted with candles—six of them! There were six candles because Mr. Franklin made candles. Other tradesmen couldn't afford to burn more than one.

All the young Franklins thought it was wonderful to have so much light, but only one of the children noticed the wonderful things the candlelight did. That child was the handsome little Benjamin, sitting close to his father.

He was only eight years old, but his keen eyes noticed how the light shone on the pewter milk jugs and spoons. He noticed how the candlelight made the earthen porridge bowls a deeper red, the tureen a dazzling white, and the mush a mound of gold.

He could see the six lights in the table, too. Its polished wood made a mirror for the lights.

It was a beautiful sight, the boy thought, and he loved it. This kitchen wasn't just the back room of a poor tradesman's home to him. It was a wonderful place, warm and bright.

Outside the windows was the world of strangers. Inside were the Franklins with their lively talk and their deep love for one another.

LIVELY TALK

The Franklins always had so much to talk about. There were the ships sailing away loaded with furs. There were the ships coming in loaded with new settlers. There were the Negro men who worked for the rich merchants. There were the sailors from all countries. There was the great new church they were going to build. There was the new lighthouse already begun.

This evening the talk was about an Indian hunter, Brown Beaver, and the great bundle of furs he had brought in this very day. There was much guessing as to how much money he had made and whether he had been cheated.

John, now twenty-four, seemed to know more about this than anyone. He was the oldest son at home and helped his father in the shop.

"I don't think anyone could cheat Brown Beaver," said John. "That Indian is very smart. He speaks English, too. He came in the shop today to buy soap."

Then John smiled and looked at Ben and smiled again.

"Well, what's the joke?" asked Peter, the next oldest boy. He was twenty-two and helped in the shop. He had been out delivering candles.

"Brown Beaver thinks Ben would make a good Indian," said John.

"What!" exclaimed Mrs. Franklin. She seemed to be frightened.

Mr. Franklin looked at John gravely.

"Yes," John went on, "he said Ben was smart for eight years old—very smart like Indian boy."

"How did he know anything about Ben?" asked Mrs. Franklin.

"He was talking to Ben outside," said John.

Everyone looked at Ben.

"I just asked him some things," said Ben.

"What things, Ben?" asked his mother.

"I asked him how many children he had, and how many bears he had killed, and how many beaver skins he had sold, and which he'd rather hunt—buffalo or deer."

"Are you sure that's all?" asked John, smiling.

Ben smiled, too, but he didn't answer.

"Was that all, Ben?" his mother asked.

"Well, I just said I'd like to go to his wigwam with him sometime," Ben admitted.

"Ben," said Mrs. Franklin sharply, "you are old enough to know better. Two boys tried to join the Indians this fall. Hunters found them in the forest later on. Both were dead."

"I know, Mother, but I'm sure the Indians didn't kill those boys," Ben replied.

"Why are you sure of that?" his father asked.

"Well, Brown Beaver wouldn't kill any boy. He told me he likes boys."

"Does that prove that the other braves are like him? You should know it doesn't. Yet you were willing to go to their camp," his father added.

"I just wanted to stay two or three days, Father. I wanted to see their houses and beds and watch the braves make arrows, and——"

His father interrupted, "What if the chief didn't want you? He has no love for white people. What if he ordered you to leave?"

"Then Brown Beaver would bring me back," Ben answered confidently.

"The chief might forbid anyone to help you. He'd send you into the forest alone."

"You couldn't find your way home, Ben," John put in seriously.

"A wild animal might attack you," Peter added.

"A bear!" exclaimed eleven-year-old Thomas.

Six-year-old Lydia began to sob. "Don't go away, Bennie," she said.

He patted her cheek fondly.

"Another thing might happen," Mrs. Franklin suggested. "If the chief thought you were smart enough to make a good hunter, he'd let you stay, Ben. But he'd hide you where no white man could ever find you."

"Wouldn't he let me go to you, Father?"

"Not even if I took an army of soldiers with me. Indian scouts would see us on the way and warn their camp. By the time we arrived the whole tribe would be gone, and you with them."

"I won't go with Brown Beaver. I won't go even if he asks me," Ben promised.

"Not even if you want to find out things?"

"No, Father, I promise you. I promise you, too, Mother," Ben added.

"It's best not to talk to strangers," Mr. Franklin explained quietly.

"Yes, sir," said Ben, "but they always tell me things I like to know."

Then supper was over and the candles were put out, all but one. The Franklins had to save even on the candles they made.

Mrs. Franklin looked at the log in the fireplace. It wouldn't last much longer.

"There's no use burning up any more wood tonight," she said. "We'll go to bed earlier."

They had to save on firewood, too. The forest was now far away from the city, and wood cost more than it used to cost.

"Then we will have our evening prayers now," said Mr. Franklin.

He opened the big Bible and began to read.

BEN IS DIFFERENT

The next morning Mr. Franklin went about his work as usual, but he couldn't keep his mind on it. He kept thinking of Ben's words—"They tell me things I like to know."

Then he remembered how Ben would leave his playmates and come into the shop to hear the talk of certain customers—soldiers, sailors and fur traders. His other sons didn't take much interest in the talk of strangers.

But Ben was different. He was so different he didn't seem to belong to the same family.

21

Ben loved to read. The other children seldom looked at a book.

Ben had learned to read by himself. He had read books when he was five years old. Now he could read the Bible.

He liked to talk about the books he had read. He didn't forget anything—not any part of any book nor anything anyone did.

The others forgot everything. They couldn't tell what they had read the week before.

Ben was interested in animals, stones, plants, clouds, and everything he saw.

His brothers weren't interested in anything except having fun after work hours.

"Ben is hungry for knowledge," Mr. Franklin thought. "I wish I could afford to send him to school. He would try at school."

Mr. Franklin and his two older sons, John and Peter, worked from daylight till dark. There was much work for them in the shop.

Thomas, who was eleven, ran errands and helped Peter deliver candles and soap.

With all that help, Mr. Franklin made barely enough to keep his large family in food and clothing. There was no money left to pay a schoolmaster or buy school books.

Mrs. Franklin had taught the older girls, Mary and Sarah, to cook, sew, spin, and weave— all the things girls needed to know.

Ben wasn't old enough to work, and he was too smart to be idle. His parents didn't know what to do about him.

"Abiah," said Mr. Franklin one day, "of all the boys in Boston, Ben is the one who should be in school. I doubt if any boy his age can read as well as he does."

"I wish you could afford it, Josiah."

"I could if I could sell the candles for the night watch, but some other candlemaker always gets the order."

"Well," said Mrs. Franklin, "we'll train Ben at home the best we can. We'll teach him to be honest, saving, and well-mannered."

"Later," said Mr. Franklin, "we'll put him into some trade. That is all we can do, Abiah."

"It's all any parents can do, if they are as poor as we are, Josiah."

The Rule

IT WAS "Story Night" in the Franklin home. Once each week the young Franklins took turns telling a story. It could be sad or funny. It could be an adventure on land or sea. It could not be a story they had read or heard. Whoever told the story had to make it up.

Supper was over. The long table had been cleared. The six candles still burned, and a new log had been put on the fire.

Then Mr. Franklin spoke. "Whose turn is it to tell the story tonight?"

"Ben's!" cried several Franklins.

"We are ready, Ben," said Mr. Franklin.

Ben went at once to the fireplace and sat on a stool, facing the others. He began his story:

"It happened this morning," said Ben. "I was playing in front of the shop when along came Ebenezer Zeezer."

"Who?" asked John and Peter.

"Who?" asked Lydia.

"Ebenezer Zeezer," Ben repeated, just as if it were actually true.

The others laughed. They knew he had made up the very amusing name.

"Ebenezer has a grandmother right here in Boston," Ben said, "over in Milk Street. Every time she goes to see Ebenezer's mother, she gives him cakes, and honey, and everything.

"She won't let his folks whip him, either—not while she's around.

"Ebenezer said he wished she lived with them all the time. He would do just what he pleased. His folks wouldn't dare to touch him."

Mrs. Franklin smiled. "I'm glad your grand-mother lives in Nantucket," she said. "I'm glad Nantucket is an island and too far from Boston for your grandmother to swim here."

Everyone laughed at that, except Lydia and Jane. They were too young to understand their mother's joke.

"Well," Ben continued, "as I said before, along came Ebenezer, but he didn't act the same. He didn't whistle, and he didn't tag me, or chase me, or anything.

"So I looked straight at him, and I saw what was the matter. He had been crying.

"What made you cry, Ebenezer?" I asked.

" 'My mother will whip me,' he said. 'I'm afraid to go home.'

" 'What did you do?' I asked.

" 'I was sent for a pennyworth of vinegar,' he said, 'and I have broken the glass and spilled the vinegar. I know Mother will whip me.'

"Then he began to cry again.

" 'She won't whip you,' I said.

" 'Oh yes, she will,' he said.

" 'Oh no, she won't,' I said.

" 'Oh yes, she will,' he said."

"That's enough of that," said Mr. Franklin. "Go on with your story."

"Well," said Ben, "Ebenezer just went on crying, and he wouldn't go home.

"Then all at once I remembered something.

" 'Ebenezer,' I said, 'I *know* your mother won't whip you.'

" 'Why won't she?' he asked.

" 'Why, because your grandmother has just gone to your house,' I said. 'I saw her go in as I came by.'

" 'Did you honest?' he asked.

" 'Honest,' I said.

" 'Honest Injun?' he asked.

" 'Honest Injun,' I said.

"Then Ebie stopped crying right away and laughed out loud. " 'Ha, ha!' he said. 'Ha, ha!'

"With that Ebenezer Zeezer went on home and was seen no more."

All the Franklins laughed at Ben's story. How they did enjoy that handsome young Benjamin who was always making up funny things!

BEN'S MISTAKE

More than two weeks had passed. Again the Franklins were sitting down to supper.

The mush was in the big white tureen, but it didn't look just right, Ben thought. The mush was not yellow enough.

It couldn't be the fault of the meal—that was as yellow as yellow could be.

It couldn't be the fault of the stirring, for his mother had stirred it as long as usual. He had wanted to help, but she wouldn't let him.

29

"You aren't old enough," said Lydia.

"I know how to stir mush," said Ben.

"Well, then, you aren't tall enough," said Thomas importantly.

Ben was short for his age. He always sat on an extra-high stool at the table, so he could see his mother plainly when she began to serve the mush. He noticed the way it dropped from the ladle. At once he knew what was wrong.

Then it was that Ben made his mistake. He knew better, but he forgot.

"Mother," he said, "don't you think the mush is a little too thin?"

Everyone stared at him. No one said a word, but Ben knew what he had done. He had broken *The Rule*.

At the Franklin table no one was allowed to talk about the food. It was bad manners to make any remark—whether the soup was thin or thick, whether the meat was raw or burned, whether the

fruit was sour or sweet, whether the pie was pumpkin or squash.

"I'm sorry, Mother," Ben said. "I'm sorry, Father, I should not have said anything."

"You must be so sorry it won't happen again," said Mr. Franklin. "Go to bed at once. Take this candle and go to your room."

Josiah Franklin always meant what he said, so Ben obeyed without one word. He left the room with the candle and climbed the narrow stairs to the second floor.

Then he passed through his mother's room. The trundle bed was pulled out from under the big bed, and the soft wool covers were turned back, ready for the little girls, Lydia and Jane.

It hadn't been very long since he had slept in this trundle bed himself. He almost wished he might sleep there tonight.

Now he was sleeping with John, Peter, and Thomas in the attic room on the third floor.

It was icy cold up there and dark. One candle didn't light up the corners. He could see those black shadows now. They looked like Indians with tomahawks. All kinds of things could be under the big beds. He'd be afraid to look. He didn't like to go up there alone in the daytime. He had never been there alone at night.

Ben looked at that nice soft trundle bed again.

"I might just rest here a little while," he thought. "It's warmer and closer to the folks. I can go upstairs before they come to bed."

He put the candlestick down on his mother's bureau. He started to lie down, but he didn't. He just stood there thinking.

"Father told me to go to my room," he said to himself. "He didn't mean this room."

Then he took up the candlestick and climbed the steep stairs to the cold attic room.

"Oh!" he thought. "Oh, how I wish I had a grandmother here, like Ebenezer Zeezer!"

Guests at the Blue Ball

MR. AND MRS. FRANKLIN had said they would teach Ben at home the best they could. Now they had begun.

Josiah and Abiah Franklin had a sort of school in the kitchen, but school was not held every day. The school, too, was not just for Ben alone. It was for all the Franklin children.

It was more like a party than a school. A guest was invited to supper, and this guest was the teacher that evening.

But the guests didn't know they were teaching! Mr. Franklin managed that. He kept them talking about their travels, or books they had read, or whatever they knew or did that was worth while for the children to learn.

If they got off the track and started to talk about foolish things, Mr. Franklin soon led them back. He was determined his children should gain knowledge from the visitors.

Abiah Franklin was determined, too. No mush-and-milk suppers for this company. She would get up a fine meal. That meant cooking at a fireplace over a hot fire and bending over pots and skillets until her back ached. Since it was for her children, she never complained.

One guest was a merchant who talked about honesty. "A man has to be honest," he said, "if he wants the respect of others."

He said also, "A small beginning as a small tradesman may in time make a rich merchant."

"Little strokes fell great oaks," he said.

"But you have to work hard," he added. "You cannot stop to play."

"The sleeping fox catches no poultry."

One day the guest was a farmer. He told them about a neighbor who was always "talking big" about the crops he was going to have. But he was too lazy to plow a large field.

"The worst wheel of the cart makes the most noise," said the farmer.

Then came a rich man who had once been a very poor man.

"Children," he said, "you must save every penny if you want to be rich. You must also save time, for time is as valuable as money.

"Early to bed and early to rise
  Makes a man healthy, wealthy, and wise."

Now Mrs. Franklin had noticed that some of the children didn't always listen to these guests. There was only one child she could count on— Ben. Weeks after, he could repeat what this guest or that guest had said.

Mr. Franklin had noticed this, too. "Ben is

the only one of our children who really wants to learn," he said one day. "He should go to school."

"Ben is going to school now," said Mrs. Franklin, "and he is learning fast."

A JOKE ON FATHER

One evening the Franklin boys had just come into the kitchen.

"Boys," said their mother, "clean up extra well, please. An old friend will be here for supper, Mr. Louis Patten, the fur trader. He's just back from Canada."

Ben was delighted. Now he would hear stories about hunting and trapping.

Mrs. Franklin wore her best dress and looked so pretty they all noticed it. The girls all wore their best dresses and looked very pretty, too.

"Be sure to listen," said Mrs. Franklin. "Mr.

Patten will tell you all about Canada. It will be a splendid lesson in geography."

Then Mr. Franklin came into the kitchen with his old friend, Louis Patten.

Ben was surprised. He expected to see a dark man with keen black eyes and jet-black hair, like those French fur traders in his father's shop. But her was a short fat man with blue eyes and light hair. He was lively, too. He was laughing with Mrs. Franklin, hugging Lydia, and kissing little Jane. Then he was smiling at all of them as they took their places at the table.

"Ah!" cried this jolly man. "It does my eyes good to see so many handsome children! Alas, I had only dogs for company there two years."

"They carried you far into the wilderness, I suppose?" asked Mr. Franklin.

"Oh, yes, yes indeed!" said the guest.

"What a chance Father is giving Mr. Patten!" thought smart Benjamin. "Mr. Patten doesn't

know it, but he will be teaching geography in just another minute."

Mrs. Franklin thought the same thing. What a chance for the children to hear all about this wilderness, its lakes, rivers, and mountains!

Everyone waited, but Mr. Patten said no more. He seemed to be looking at every dish of food on the table.

And then and there *The Rule* was broken.

"Abiah," said the guest, "I haven't sat down to a meal like this in two years. It gives me pleasure just to look at it."

What was this? The guest talking about food! "That will never do!" thought Mr. Franklin, so he spoke quickly.

"What kind of country did you travel through, Louis?" he asked.

"Now comes the geography," thought Ben.

But Mr. Patten only said, "Oh, it was so-so." Then he flipped his hand and was silent.

"Josiah won't give up," thought his wife.

Josiah didn't give up. "What kind of a trip did you have over the mountains?" he asked. He was determined to get some geography out of his friend.

But again Mr. Patten flipped his hand and said, "Oh, only so-so."

Then he gazed at the roast goose which Mr. Franklin was carving. Suddenly he turned to Mrs. Franklin.

"Abiah!" he said. "I have never seen a better-browned goose. The very odor is delicious."

"Thank you," said Abiah.

Josiah now saw a good chance for a nature lesson. "There are many wild geese in Canada, I believe."

"Thousands—millions," said Mr. Patten. Then he stopped.

Again everyone waited. There was not another word from Louis.

"Could you tell the children something about their habits?" asked Mr. Franklin.

"Sorry, I don't know a thing about geese. Didn't go hunting—too cold." And with that he shuddered just to think of it.

By this time he had been served and had begun eagerly to eat.

"Ah!" he cried. "Never have I eaten such goose, so tender, so juicy, so sweet! This dressing, too, is delicious! Do tell me what you put into it, Abiah?"

"Chestnuts," said Mrs. Franklin. She didn't want to talk about food, but she had to answer the man or seem impolite.

"Is that all? Didn't you use a bit of sage?"

"Oh, yes, just a bit," said Abiah.

"There seems to be another flavor, too. Oh! I have it now!" cried the delighted visitor. "It's apple, isn't it?"

"Yes," said Abiah. "I forgot that."

Josiah decided to stop this foolish talk about food. "Louis," he said, "what about the Indians in Canada? Were they honest? Did you like them? Did you have trouble with them?"

"Oh, they'd be all right if they knew how to cook," said the fur trader. "The awful meals I've had to eat with them!" Again he shuddered, just to show how awful it was.

Then he talked about the gravy, the baked potatoes, the stewed corn, the mashed turnips, the baked squash, the pickles, the maple syrup, the wild honey, the wild-grape jam, the pumpkin pie, and the cranberry tarts.

At last Mr. Franklin gave up. He didn't ask another question.

That night after Mr. Patten had gone, Mr. Franklin said, "Well, you can lead a horse to water, but you can't make him drink."

"I noticed it," said Mrs. Franklin, and she smiled knowingly.

The children who understood smiled, too. Those who didn't understand smiled anyway.

"The joke is on me," said Father, "so I'll pay. I'll give you a bit of music."

Then he played his violin and sang. That pleased the whole family, for Father had a good voice. So the evening ended happily after all.

Grandfather Peter Folger

It was a cold winter in Boston, the coldest in many years, but soap and candles had to be made and delivered.

Peter and Thomas looked like bears when they went out, they wore so much clothing.

The younger children, Jane, Lydia, Ben, stayed at home close to the fire.

After her morning work was done, Mrs. Franklin would sit close to the fire, too. She would take up her knitting, but she was never too busy to talk to her children.

"I do believe," she said one morning, "yes, I'm sure, it was just as cold as it is today—the day your grandfather finished my favorite little red wool dress."

"Did he sew it?" asked Lydia.

Ben had to smile. The idea of Grandfather Peter Folger sewing seemed very funny!

"He wove it, Lydia," said Mother. "He wove the cloth from which we made my dress and all our clothing. He wove for the neighbors, too. In fact, people all over Nantucket wanted Father to do their weaving."

"He must have been a good weaver," said Ben.

"He was, but he couldn't make a living. So many people couldn't pay for their cloth after he had woven it. The whalers had a poor catch that year. You see, children, the Nantucket people are whalers, almost all of them."

"Grandfather wasn't a whaler, was he?" asked Ben thoughtfully.

"No," said Mrs. Franklin, "but he could do almost any kind of work. He was an educated

man, too. So next, he became a teacher, and I went to his school."

"Did you mind him?" asked Jane.

"Indeed I did. I was sorry when I had to stop school. It closed in a month or so—the people were too poor to pay the master."

"No whales again?" asked Ben.

Mrs. Franklin nodded. "Another poor catch," she said. "So Father had to give up teaching, too, and find something else to do.

"Then he bought a mill and ground corn for everyone on the island, even the Indians."

"How could he talk to them?" asked Ben.

"He learned their language, and they found they could trust him." said Mrs. Franklin, "Father made some money that year, but the next summer there was no rain. The streams dried up and soon there wasn't even enough water to turn the mill wheel."

"Oh dear!" said Ben.

"Yes, it was too bad, but it wasn't long until he was doing some work he loved. He was surveying land for new settlers. That means, children, that he measured it. Now this land was in the woods, so of course Father had to live there in a camp.

48

"He had a helper, and the Indians were friendly so he got along very well for some time."

"*Some time!*" Smart little Benjamin noticed that at once. "Did something happen?"

"I'll tell you about that tomorrow. I must get dinner now," said Mrs. Franklin.

"When I grow up," said Ben to his sisters, "I'm going to do everything Grandfather did."

"Will you be a weaver?" asked Lydia.

"I will. And I'll be a teacher, and a miller, and a surveyor."

"Will you live in the woods?" asked Jane.

"Yes," said Ben firmly, "and I'll learn the Indian language, too."

How proud they were of Ben! Lydia told the big boys that night what Ben planned to do.

"Ha, ha!" laughed John. "So you're going to learn four trades, are you! It's all I can do to learn one."

"I haven't learned one yet," Peter said.

"I am afraid I will never learn the candle and soap trade," said Thomas.

"Never mind, Ben," said sweet Abiah Franklin. "Maybe you'll surprise your big brothers one of these days."

THE INDIAN GIRL AND THE PONY

The next day it was still very cold, and the children still huddled over the fire.

Again Mother sat close to the children and took up her knitting.

"Mother, you promised to tell us what happened to Grandfather," said Ben.

"Oh, yes, so I did. Well, one day a pretty little Indian girl, about fourteen, came to Father's camp in the woods. She wanted him to pull a tooth. She said the Medicine Man had gone hunting, and she couldn't wait for him, because her tooth was hurting so badly.

50

Then Mother told the following story about her father and the Indians:

Father pulled her tooth and she went away.

Early the next morning the girl came again, leading a beautiful little pony.

"For you—for tooth," she told Father.

"No," said Father, "I can't take such a fine gift from you. Keep your pony."

But the girl only laughed and ran quickly into the forest.

That afternoon the Medicine Man came to Father's camp. He was very angry.

"The pony is mine," he said.

"Take it, then," said Father.

The Indian took the pony, but he scowled as he went away.

Father was worried. He couldn't risk having trouble with the Indians.

"Did he have trouble?" Ben asked quickly.

"Wait," said his mother. "You will see."

Now the very next morning here came the girl again with the same pony.

"For you," she said, and ran away.

That afternoon here came the Medicine Man again. He was so angry he didn't say one word. He leaped on the pony and started away.

Suddenly he stopped and shot an arrow into the tree by which Father was standing.

Shooting the arrow was a warning that he would shoot Father next time.

About a week later the Indian girl came again. This time she came, with the same pony.

Before she could speak, quick as a wildcat, Father seized her arm.

"Take me to your camp," he said. "Take me to your father."

She shook her head, but Father was so fierce she had to obey him.

Just before they reached the Indian village, she said, "Wait, I bring him."

So Father waited, but he held his musket ready to shoot.

Pretty soon here came the girl with a big brave. "Chief Red Wolf," she said. "He is my father."

Father explained everything to the chief. He told him he didn't want the pony. He had only wanted to help the girl.

The chief turned to his daughter. "Bright Star," he said, "why you take pony not yours?"

"Medicine Man no pay white man," said Bright Star.

"Why should he pay me?" asked Father.

"You pull—he no pull," said Bright Star.

"Oh!" said Father. "You think he should pay me for pulling your tooth?"

"Yes, yes!" cried Bright Star. "I think it!"

"And so," Father went on, "you bring me his pony to pay his debt?"

"Yes, yes, I do!" she cried again.

The chief's eyes were twinkling. "How many times you give pony, Bright Star?"

"Three times I give pony to man. Two times he get it back!"

The chief laughed. Bright Star laughed. Father laughed.

Then Red Wolf said he would tell the Medicine Man how it happened.

"So now," Red Wolf said to Father, "take the pony. The pony is yours."

Father took the pony and brought it home with him. Then I learned to ride it and had wonderful times riding it about the neighborhood."

Boston School

SPRING HAD come, and Ben was playing out-doors again. He did not see the grand coach that drove up to the Blue Ball one day, nor did he see the three grand gentlemen who got out of the coach and went into the shop.

Mr. Franklin was astonished. He knew these men were important persons in Boston. One man was a judge. Another man was a doctor. The third man was a leading merchant.

"Why have they come here?" he thought. "Such grand gentlemen do not come for candles or soap. They would send their servants." But he bowed and greeted them politely.

"Mr. Franklin," said the judge, "we wish to speak with you alone."

Josiah led the gentlemen to the kitchen. They bowed to Mrs. Franklin, and then sat, stiff and straight, on benches.

Abiah went to a far corner with her knitting. She knew they had not come to talk with her.

Josiah stood on the hearth and faced the visitors. He still wore his big leather "boiling" apron and his huge, white "pouring" cap.

"Mr. Franklin," said the judge, "we are the Select Men. As you know, we are selected by the Governor to go to and fro through the city to see if parents are doing their duty."

"Yes, Your Honor," said Josiah.

The judge continued, "The new law says that every child, boy or girl, must learn to read. If any parent refuses to obey, he will be fined or sent to jail."

"Also," said the doctor, "this new law says that

his child, or children, can be taken from him and given to someone who will give them schooling."

Josiah was alarmed. He hadn't heard about this new law. Abiah was frightened, too. What would these men do? Would they take any of their children?

"Mr. Franklin," said the merchant, "you have children of school age, but they are not in school. Can you explain this?"

"Yes, gentlemen," said Josiah, "I can. Some of them have gone to a Dame School."

"That is according to the law," said the judge. "We approve the Dame Schools even though they are taught by women in their own homes."

"And my three older boys are learning my trade," continued Josiah.

"That also is according to the law," said the judge. "Learning a trade is schooling."

"What about your youngest son, Benjamin?" asked the doctor.

"I can't afford to send him to school. My family is so large now I can't even pay the small fee at a Dame School."

"But the Boston Latin School is free," the doctor explained.

"Pardon me, sir, but the books aren't free," said Josiah. "And each pupil has to pay his share for the firewood burned."

"Ah, but that is so little!" The rich merchant sounded surprised.

"It is not little for me," said Josiah.

There was silence for a moment. Then the judge spoke. "I have heard that Benjamin can read the Bible. Is this true?"

"It is true," said Josiah.

"And he is only eight years old?"

"He was eight last January, sir. He was born in 1706."

The judge turned to the other Select Men. "That is remarkable, gentlemen. What a fine scholar the boy would make! He might even become a minister in the church."

"Do you hear that, Mr. Franklin?" asked the doctor. "To have a son in the church would be a great honor."

But Josiah Franklin shook his head. "I cannot let the others want, that one may go to school," he said.

The Select Men looked at one another and nodded slowly.

"Mr. Franklin," said the judge, "we believe you. Would it help if the city should order your candles for the night watch for their lanterns?"

"Yes," said Josiah, "I could then send Ben to school. I thank you for your kindness."

The visitors stood and bowed to Mrs. Franklin. Mr. Franklin opened the door into the shop. They left the kitchen, and he followed them.

"God be praised!" said Abiah. "Ben will be a minister after all."

The candles had been sold to the night watch, and Ben had been sent to school, a school that lasted the year round. There was no summer vacation. There was one holiday for Thanksgiving and one for Christmas.

The opening bell rang at 8 A.M. in the winter, but at 7 A.M. in the summer. The dismissal bell rang at 4 P.M. in winter, but at 5 P.M. in summer.

Girls were not allowed to attend the Boston Latin School at all. All the teachers were men, and they were very strict. The boys were whipped for the least thing—even a mistake in their regular lessons.

The books weren't even written in English. They were written in Latin, the language used long ago in Rome.

In those days people thought every preacher should know Latin, at least know enough to say a few Latin sentences.

So, since Ben was to be a preacher, he must study this language and go to this Latin School.

There was no spelling or writing or arithmetic. There was no music or drawing or shopwork. There was just Latin!

The pupils studied Latin all morning. From eleven to twelve was their dinner hour. From twelve until one they were questioned about last Sunday's sermon at church. Then all the afternoon they studied Latin again.

Ben began his studies with *Aesop's Fables*. The book was written in Latin, and he had to learn the fables by heart.

Every boy was learning something by heart. Almost all of the boys didn't know what the verse or story meant. They were just learning to say the words.

The school should have been called the "Boston Parrot School."

Ben had been going two months and had

learned to repeat in Latin one fable, "The Dog and His Shadow."

The master was pleased. "You shall say that fable next month on Visitation Day," he said.

Visitation Day was the day for the yearly visit of the Governor and the important men of Boston. Many fathers would come. The Select Men would be there, too.

The boys would speak their Latin pieces. And woe to the boy who failed! He would be whipped severely after the visitors left.

Ben's best friend in school was a boy three years older, Nathan Morse. Nathan had to learn the fable of "The Wolf and the Kid," but he just couldn't remember the Latin words.

Ben helped him so much he learned this fable himself and could say it better than Nathan.

"If I fail on Visitation Day," said Nathan, "I don't know what I will do. My father will feel very bad. He wants me to be a minister so much he is going hungry to keep me in the Latin School. I must not fail."

After that, Ben helped his friend, morning, noon, and night. At last Nathan could give "The Wolf and the Kid" without a single mistake. Ben was as happy about Nathan's learning his fable as Nathan himself.

VISITATION DAY

Then came the great day, October 10, 1714. The visitors came at ten o'clock in the morning. There were fifty of them, and they were all men.

There was the Governor in his velvet suit, powdered wig, and hat with feathers.

There were preachers in black robes.

Judges and lawyers came in black robes and powdered wigs.

There were doctors and merchants, wearing fine clothes and shoes with silver buckles.

Rich fathers, dressed in satin suits with lace ruffles, came in fine coaches.

There were only two poor fathers. They were back in a corner. They wore no silver buckles, no fine wigs, and no fine feathers.

Ben's keen eyes found these two men. "There's your father and mine!" he whispered to Nathan.

Both boys were delighted, but they were so frightened their knees were shaking. Nathan was almost ill from fright.

All the boys were scared, and their schoolmaster was scared, too. Woe to him if the boys forgot! He might lose his school.

Ben was to speak first because he was the youngest boy. He wore his Sunday clothes, a blue wool suit with brass buttons, and he looked more handsome than ever.

He heard his name called, and he went to the platform. He bowed to the Governor and then to the master. Then he heard the master say that

Ben Franklin would give the fable of "The Wolf and the Kid."

Quick as a flash Ben knew what had happened. "The master doesn't know he has given me Nathan's fable," he thought. "What shall I do? If I say it, Nathan will get into trouble. If I tell them it isn't my piece, the master will get into trouble.

"Well, I won't speak Nathan's fable, and I won't tell on the master," Ben said to himself.

So the brave little boy just stood there and looked at the floor.

"They'll make him say it," thought poor Nathan. "Then what will I do?"

"We are waiting, Benjamin," the Governor said. "Say your piece, please."

Benjamin just stood there and looked at the the floor. He could not say either his fable or Nathan's fable without hurting someone.

"Well," said His Honor after a minute or two,

"it is plain to us all that you do not know this fable. You have been too lazy to learn it."

The Select Men nodded their heads. The preachers and judges and doctors and lawyers nodded their heads. The merchants and rich fathers nodded their heads.

The Governor went on talking to Ben. "When I was a lad, I could say a dozen fables in Latin. I am not pleased with you, my boy. Master Williams, you should punish him severely."

"Yes, Your Honor," said the master.

"A good whipping will take the stubbornness out of him," continued the Governor.

"Yes, indeed!" said the lawyers.

"Yes, indeed!" said the preachers.

"Yes, indeed!" said the others.

No, not all the others. Two fathers in a far corner didn't agree with the Governor. They knew Ben wasn't just being stubborn. They knew it was all the master's fault.

Alas, the master still did not know what a mistake he had made. He knew Ben was frightened, but "that doesn't excuse him," he thought. "The boy could have said a line or two instead of just standing there like a ninny looking at the floor."

There was anger in his eyes as he looked at Ben. "Go to your seat," he said sharply.

Ben went to his seat, a badly frightened little boy. He knew he would be punished.

Then Nathan's name was called, but Nathan did not stand. Instead, Mr. Morse rose in that far corner.

"Nathan is ill," he said. "I am taking him home, right now."

For a few minutes there was talking and confusion as Mr. Morse took Nathan away. So no one noticed Josiah Franklin go up to the platform and speak with Master Williams.

"You don't understand about Ben," he said in

a low voice. "He was only trying to help his friend Nathan."

"Help Nathan!" exclaimed the master. "What do you mean? How could Ben's refusing to speak help Nathan?"

"You announced the wrong fable, Master Williams! You said Ben would give 'The Wolf and the Kid.' That was Nathan's fable."

The master's face became as white as chalk. "Oh!" he said. "Did I do that?"

"You did indeed, sir," said Mr. Franklin. "That's what made Nathan ill. That's why Ben wouldn't speak."

"I'm glad you told me, Mr. Franklin. To tell you the truth, I don't know what I said. I've never been so upset. I didn't expect so many visitors to come today."

"One such as the Governor would be too many," said Josiah.

"S-sh!" whispered the master, but he smiled

and seemed to be pleased. Then he became serious again. "What can I do to make things right?" he asked. "I'll go to see Nathan, of course. But what can I do for Ben?"

"Just don't whip him," said Josiah.

"Of course I won't. Your boy helped me as much as he helped Nathan. If he had said one word—if he had told the Governor it wasn't his piece, I'd be dismissed from the school."

"That is very likely," said Josiah.

"It took courage to do what your son did today, Mr. Franklin. There isn't another boy in Boston with such character. I shall give him a present— a bag of sugar plums. But don't tell the Governor, please!"

"I won't'" said Josiah. "The Governor knows too much now—too much Latin!"

The master smiled. Josiah smiled. Then a little boy in a blue suit with brass buttons knew that all was well, and he smiled too.

It was now a year later, October, 1715. Ben was no longer in the Boston Latin School. His father had changed his mind about making him a minister. It would take too long and cost too much. Besides, he wondered if Latin was all Ben ought to know.

Mr. Morse thought the same thing and took Nathan out of the Boston Latin School, too.

The two boys were sent to a Writing School. That was what this school was called, but reading, spelling, and arithmetic were also taught. These subjects seemed more useful than Latin.

It was a pay school, but the fee was less than the books and firewood at the Latin School.

The writing master was a beautiful writer. He made his own copybooks, and the pupils tried to imitate his writing. Each pupil had a copybook that only he was to use.

A half day would be spent on one writing lesson of only ten lines. That was just one page in the copybook.

Ben learned to write a clear and beautiful handwriting.

He learned to make goose-quill pens and ink. He made an inkwell out of a cow's horn. One end of the horn was sawed off and then fitted into a wooden base.

The master was pleased with Ben's reading and spelling. But Ben didn't get along as well in arithmetic as he did in other subjects.

There were no arithmetic books for the pupils. The master wrote a problem on a boy's slate and told him to work it.

Sometimes it would take a boy three or four days to get one problem. If he asked for help the master would say, "I haven't time to help you."

And he didn't. There were so many pupils and so many classes he couldn't help each child. He didn't have time to explain "carrying" in addition. He just told Ben to do it. Ben did. But his slate looked like this:

$$
\begin{array}{r}
7\ \ 2\ \ 5 \\
+\ 6\ \ 9\ \ 8 \\
\hline
13\ \ 11\ \ 13
\end{array}
\qquad
\begin{array}{r}
8\ \ 4\ \ 8 \\
+\ 2\ \ 6\ \ 2 \\
\hline
10\ \ 10\ \ 10
\end{array}
$$

It looked like this when the master marked it:

$$
\begin{array}{r}
7\ \ 2\ \ 5 \\
+\ 6\ \ 9\ \ 8 \\
\hline
13\ \ 11\ \ 13 \ \times
\end{array}
\qquad
\begin{array}{r}
8\ \ 4\ \ 8 \\
+\ 2\ \ 6\ \ 2 \\
\hline
10\ \ 10\ \ 10 \ \times
\end{array}
\qquad 0
$$

Ben couldn't understand this zero grade. He showed his slate to Nathan at noon. "I'm sure the answers are right," he declared. "I've counted them on my fingers four times."

Nathan looked over the problems. Then he said, "I don't see anything wrong with the answers. That's the way I added my sums."

"Let's ask the teacher," Ben suggested.

"I'm afraid to," answered Nathan.

"He won't whip us for asking. This is a good time. The afternoon classes haven't begun. I'm not afraid. Are you really?"

"No, indeed!" Nathan now stated.

But four knees were shaking by the time the boys reached the master's desk, and the hands that held the slates were trembling.

The master was busy marking a pile of slates.

"Please, sir, would you look at our sums?" Ben asked. "I can't find my mistake."

"I can't find mine either," Nathan said.

"I marked your slates, didn't I?" the teacher answered crossly.

"Yes, sir," the boys replied.

"I haven't time to look at them again. Can't you see I'm busy?"

"Yes, sir."

"Then go to your seats, and don't bother me again," the master commanded the boys.

Every day Nathan and Ben received zero in

addition, for they still did not know how they had to carry.

Subtraction was even worse. "It was a strange thing," Ben thought, "to subtract from no ones and get nine ones. Or from no tens and get nine tens. Like this:

$$
\begin{array}{r} 1\ 0\ 0 \\ -\quad\ 1 \\ \hline 9\ 9 \end{array}
\qquad
\begin{array}{r} 1\ 0\ 0 \\ -\ 1\ 0 \\ \hline 9\ 0 \end{array}
$$

A good teacher could have taught that in five minutes: how to take from the hundreds to get ten tens, and then how to take from the ten tens to get ten ones. But Ben's master just let his class think those ten tens and ten ones come down from a blue sky.

It didn't seem to make any difference to Nathan and the other boys. They didn't care where they came from.

But Ben had a different kind of mind. He had

to know the reason for everything. Those tens and ones must come from somewhere. He was puzzled and confused. He knew he would fail in subtraction, and he did. Then, of course, he couldn't do division, long or short.

At first the boys teased him. They even made up some rhymes.

"Take 9 from nothing, little Ben,
Take 9 from nothing: you'll get ten."

"Poor Ben was very sad.
He couldn't subtract, he couldn't add.
He couldn't divide, long or short—
But aside from that he was very smart."

Ben was smart. He read every book in the school's small library. The other boys couldn't read some of them at all.

After a while they stopped teasing Ben. Instead, they came to him for help with their reading, spelling, and compositions—everything in fact, except arithmetic.

Swimming at High Bank

BEN HELPED the boys in another way, too—he taught many of them to swim. He was the best swimmer in the Writing School. Some of the boys said he was the best swimmer in Boston, and he was only ten years old.

Ben couldn't remember when he had learned.

"Maybe I was six years old," he said. "My father taught me to swim, but I learned the fancy strokes by myself—no, not really by myself."

You see Ben was honest. He didn't want to pretend things that weren't quite true. He told the boys about reading a book on swimming with pictures of fancy strokes.

He said he studied these pictures and then practiced them in water until he could do them.

He was very strong and could swim as well in fresh water as in salt. The river or the ocean— it made no difference to him.

None of his friends could do that. It was easier to swim in salt water, so they always went to the bay instead of the river.

But today they decided to go to the river. It was time the other boys learned to swim in fresh water, Ben said.

They went to a place called "High Bank." It was a lonesome spot. No one ever went there except the boys because the bank was so steep.

The boys were surprised presently to see a man watching them from the shore. They knew he was a sailor from his cap and his wide-at-the-ankle trousers. He watched Ben especially.

Ben noticed the man watching him. Now the sailor was calling and pointing to him.

"Come in! Come in!"

Ben swam to shore with fancy strokes.

"I've been watching you, my lad," said the sailor, "and I've a mind to learn your strokes myself. I'll pay you well for some lessons. I'm the captain of a sloop in the bay."

"I'll ask my father," said Ben.

"I've no time for that," said the captain. "I must go to my ship now. We'll swim in the bay close by."

By this time the other boys were on the shore. Like all boys all over the world, they wanted to know what was going on.

"It isn't far to my father's shop," said Ben. "I can be back in a jiffy."

"No," said the man. "I can't wait. If you want to make some money, come along now to my ship."

Ben did want to earn something. He wanted to buy that book on swimming. "I might go for a little while," he thought.

"His father won't let him go to any ship," said Nathan. "Not unless his father goes along."

That seemed to make the man angry. "Who is talking to you?" he said roughly.

Ben tried to explain. "That's because my brother Josiah ran away and went to sea."

"Oh!" said the man. "Did you ever hear from your brother?"

"No, sir," said Ben.

"Do you want me to find him?"

"His father has had a hundred sailors looking for him," Nathan put in again.

"Hold your tongue!" shouted the stranger angrily. "Get out! All of you!" But not you," he told Ben, "you stay."

Then he put one hand on Ben's shoulder and the other on the knife in his belt.

The boys were frightened. They climbed the steep bank as fast as they could, and they didn't stop until they were safe in the bushes on the top.

"I don't believe he wants to learn fancy strokes!" Nathan said in a low voice. "He just wants to get Ben on his ship and take him away. Come, quick! We'll go to the candle shop!"

HURRY, MR. FRANKLIN! HURRY!

It didn't take the boys long to reach the candle shop. "Mr. Franklin! Mr. Franklin!" they called out as they rushed through the low door.

Mr. Franklin came quickly from the back of the shop. "What is it, boys? Has anything happened to Ben?"

"There's a strange sailor talking to him!" cried Nathan. "He's trying to get Ben on his ship! He drove us away!"

"Where are they?"

"High Bank!" shouted the boys.

Mr. Franklin didn't stop to take off his cap or apron. He ran out of the shop and into the street. The boys followed him, but they couldn't keep up.

Through the narrow streets he ran, past little shops, little houses, docks, and narrow lanes. At last he reached the Charles River. High Bank was near, but it seemed a long time before he had any hope of finding Ben and the sailor.

He thought of his son Josiah as he ran—how he had run away to sea and had never been heard from since he left home.

This happened often in Boston. Evil men would coax boys away from their homes, hide them in their ships, and make them work as seamen. No one knew if they could ever come home.

"Now," Mr. Franklin thought, "they are after Ben. He is healthy and strong. He would be useful on board a ship.

"This stranger will tell Ben yarns about big fish, big storms, big fights with pirates. All of the stories are big lies, but Ben may believe him. Ben is only ten years old.

"Come to think of it, Ben is always going to the docks to see a ship come in or sail away. He seems to love the sea and boats.

"Yes, he might go with this sailor. He might run away from home. Josiah wasn't much older when he disappeared."

It hadn't taken Mr. Franklin long to think all those things. They flashed through his mind like lightning as he ran along.

Now he was at the path. It was hidden by thick bushes, but he knew where it was. He had been there many times with his boys.

Had he come in time? Was Ben still there? Quickly he parted the bushes and looked down at the shore. Yes! The sailor was still talking to young Benjamin.

Mr. Franklin went down the path. He didn't make a sound, he stepped so lightly. Now he could hear the sailor's words: "Are you going to spend your life in this little town? There's nothing here for a smart boy like you. Get out. See the world. Go to England. Go to France and Spain and Italy. Go everywhere. That's the life, my lad!"

"Father wants me to learn a trade."

"Ho, ho!" laughed the sailor. "You won't make any money at that. I'll show you how to make a fortune."

"Why, how could I make a fortune, sir?"

"Your fancy strokes will do it for you. I'll have crowds coming to see you. I'll have you swimming before kings and queens."

"Kings and queens! Could you really do that?" Ben asked.

"Certainly. It would mean money for me, too, wouldn't it?"

"Of course," said Ben. "I wouldn't want all the money."

"You won't get a penny," the sailor said to himself. But aloud he said, "You'll be seeing the world, too. I'll take you all over Europe. You'd like that, I guess. Eh, my lad?"

"I'd like it better than anything in the world!" said Ben.

The sailor stood. Ben stood.

"Come along then. If there's a breeze, we'll sail tonight."

"But I'll have to tell my folks!"

"Tell your folks!" said the captain angrily.

"You'll not tell anyone!" He seized Ben's arm and held him. "It's no use screaming either. There's no one about to hear."

Just then a hand reached out from the thick underbrush. A strong arm followed the hand. The hand became a fist. The fist shot out like a bullet, and the sailor was knocked down flat.

Josiah Franklin followed his good strong arm and stood over the unconscious man. He drew the knife from the sailor's belt and threw it into the river nearby.

"Just so he can't use it on us before we get up the bank," said Mr. Franklin.

"I'm so glad you came, Father! I'm so glad!" said the frightened boy.

"I was just in time to save you, my son."

Ben's Experiments

FOR SOME time Ben had been wondering if there were any way to swim faster—maybe with something on his hands and feet.

This idea was like a seed planted in good soil. Slowly a picture grew in his mind—a picture of swimming shoes, or paddles.

The seed had begun to sprout.

Ben thought a long time about the size. The paddles must be neither too long nor too short, too narrow nor too wide.

The right kind of wood was important, too— neither too heavy nor too light.

At last his plans were made. He knew the size

he would make his paddles, and he had found the right kind of wood. The sprouts had become a stalk and was putting out leaves.

Mr. Franklin showed Ben how to use the tools he needed, but he let the boy do the work himself. It was Ben's first invention, and Ben wanted to make it alone.

In time the paddles were finished. The plant had bloomed!

Ben was ready to try them out, so he set the day. "Next Saturday afternoon," he said, "at four o'clock, at the big pond in Green's meadow."

All over Boston boys were talking about Ben's invention. At the Latin and Writing Schools they didn't talk about anything else.

Saturday came. In Green's meadow a hundred boys were waiting and arguing.

"The paddles won't work," said one boy.

"Yes, they will," said another. "I'd like to try them myself."

"They'll cramp his legs," said the third.

"They will not!" shouted a dozen or so.

Ben paid no attention to all this talk. He was too busy with his paddles. Nathan Morse was tying them to Ben's wrists and ankles.

The pond wasn't large enough for everyone to get close to Ben, so they had to spread out. Finally there was a circle of boys all the way around the pond.

"Why didn't Ben choose a larger pond?" they grumbled. "Or why didn't he go to the river or the bay or the creek?"

But Ben knew what he was doing. He had thought it all out carefully.

He wasn't sure the paddles would work so he wanted to try them in smooth water first. That meant choosing a small pond where there was no current. He could try the paddles in the bay later.

Now he was ready. The boys hardly dared to breathe as Ben floated out from the shore.

All around the pond boys were whispering to each other:

"What if the paddles don't work!"

"What if they cramp his legs and arms!"

"What if he goes down!"

Even Nathan was worried. He didn't take his eyes off Ben. He was ready to go to him at the first sign of trouble.

Now Ben began to paddle, slowly at first. Then he swam faster and faster until he was going through the water like a streak. Never had the boys seen such fast swimming. The paddles did work! There was no doubt of that.

So a hundred boys screamed and yelled and whooped. They jumped up and down, and just about went wild.

Even those who had said the paddles wouldn't work were just as pleased as the others and made just as much noise.

It didn't take Ben long to reach the opposite

shore. Nor did it take one hundred boys long to meet him there. Of course they all talked at once asking questions.

"Did you like it? Could you really swim faster with those paddles?"

"I did swim faster," said Ben, "but I didn't like it. The paddles hurt my wrists and ankles. They weighted me down, too."

Ben wouldn't even paddle back, but the boys didn't care. He was just as wonderful to them. He had made the paddles, and they had worked. Their friend and playmate was an inventor!

HIS SWIMMING KITE

One day the word went around that Ben Franklin would try a new experiment. It was to be at the "Big Pond," the next afternoon after school, too.

To the "Big Pond" then went half the boys of

Boston. "What is Ben going to do? Is it another invention?" But no one could answer because no one seemed to know.

When the boys arrived they saw Ben in the water close to the shore. Then they saw Nathan Morse give him a stick. Tied to this stick was the string of a large paper kite.

Ben and Nathan had made this kite. It was extra large and extra strong because it was to be used for this experiment.

Now some time before this, Ben had decided that a kite could be put to work. "It should pull something," he said to Nathan. "Why wouldn't it be better than paddles? I'd be willing to try it."

Now everything was ready for this "try-out" of a kite for swimming.

"Boys," said Nathan in a loud voice, "Ben is going to let this kite pull him across the pond. He will not take a single stroke. The pond is wide at this point."

"Which way is he going?" asked a little boy.

The big boys laughed.

"Oh, Ben!" one of them called. "Which way are you going?"

The big boys laughed again, but the little boys didn't know why.

"Will the kite bring him back to this side?" asked another little boy.

Again the big boys laughed, and one of them called, "Ben! Are you coming back this way?"

The big boys thought that was very funny, but the little boys didn't see the joke at all.

They didn't know that Ben would have to go the way the kite pulled him, and the way the kite went would depend on the wind.

Just now, the wind was from the east, so the kite would blow to the west shore. Of course the kite couldn't bring Ben back—not unless the wind changed and blew from west to east.

Now Ben let out the string. The kite flew high

in the air, and Ben began to move across the pond. He lay on his back, floating. He didn't take a single stroke.

The boys all agreed on that, for they watched very closely.

"The kite is doing it all. Ben is getting a free ride," they said.

The boys yelled and whooped and jumped up and down. Then they all raced to the opposite shore where Ben was to land.

He had barely reached the shore when they all shouted, "How was it? How did you like it?"

"It was fun," said Ben. "It was so much fun I wanted to laugh all the time."

"Do it again!" cried the boys.

"I will if this wind lasts," said Ben.

He started to walk around the pond. The boys followed and asked questions.

"Why didn't you fly the kite high all the time?" asked one.

"Because I wanted to go faster," Ben answered. "So I took in the string and lowered the kite. I felt the change right away. The pull was stronger, and I went much faster."

"I thought you were going too fast at one time," said another boy.

"I thought so myself," said Ben. "You noticed I let out the string again, didn't you?"

"I noticed the kite was flying higher," said the boy. "But did you really go slower?"

"Yes, indeed, much slower," said Ben.

"What would you do if a high wind came up?" asked a third boy.

"I'd let go of the stick pretty quick," said Ben.

By this time the boys had reached the starting point, but the wind had died down. The kite was useless.

That night all over Boston, boys told their folks about Ben Franklin's "Swimming Kite."

Sailboats

WATER, WATER, WATER! Salt water, fresh water! Creeks, rivers, bays, and the great ocean beyond! That was Boston country in 1716.

No wonder Boston boys knew how to swim and row and fish. No wonder they knew how to manage sailboats. They fairly lived on the water in the summertime.

If the father was rich, the boy would have a sailboat of his own. If the father was poor, the boy would make a boat of some kind, anything that would float.

Ben and Nathan made one—that is, they made one over. They bought an old, leaky boat from a fisherman and paid for it by mending his nets. They bought two old sails from another fisherman and paid for them the same way.

Then they went to work on repairs. This took some time because Ben was never quite satisfied. More than once Nathan thought the boat was ready to use, but Ben always found something to be improved.

You see how very careful Ben was. He wanted things exactly right not just half right.

At last Ben said he thought the boat would do, but he wouldn't take it out until his father had examined it. Mr. Franklin went over the little boat carefully. He tested seams, sails, masts, ropes, and rudder.

The boys waited anxiously. What would Mr. Franklin say?

At last he turned to them. "Boys," he said, "you have done your work well. Your boat is ready to sail."

"I'm so glad!" said Ben.

"I'm glad, too!" said Nathan.

"Why not call her *Glad?*" asked Mr. Franklin.

So *Glad* it was. All that summer the boys sailed her over bays, rivers, and creeks. The boys were not allowed to sail the *Glad* out into the great ocean.

It seemed to Ben there was no end to the things he must learn about handling a sailboat.

He must know how to change direction, of course, in order to take advantage of side winds. This was called *tacking*.

He must know how to *tack* (change the boat's course) when advancing against the wind, meet-it head-on.

Nathan was afraid to try tacking. He took charge of the rudder.

Then Ben began to understand why seamen were always talking about winds. A good sailor must know where the wind came from each month of the year. He must know when a squall was coming, for it came fast and with little warning. He must know what to do with the sails whatever happened.

There was a reason for everything that was done on a sailboat, and Ben went about finding those reasons. He read books about gales, squalls, and hurricanes. He talked with sailors and captains and asked them to show him how to handle sails.

One of these captains was Robert Holmes. He had married one of Ben's sisters, so he was Ben's brother-in-law.

"Mr. Franklin," said Captain Holmes, one day, "Ben knows as much about a boat right now as many a sailor."

The sailors began to call Ben "Skipper." This is what sailors call the captain of a vessel.

"Good morning, Skipper," they would say or, "Aye, aye, Skipper."

Nothing could have made Ben happier, not even a velvet suit or silver shoe-buckles. It was music in his ears.

BEN THE SKIPPER

One Saturday Jonathan Bell asked Ben and Nathan to go sailing with him in his new boat, *White Lily*. It was a beautiful boat. When its white sails were spread, it looked like a fairy boat flying over the blue water.

Jonathan asked the boys to steer, but he didn't offer to let them sail. He knew they wanted to, but he was selfish. He was the son of a rich merchant, and he had always had his own way.

Ben saw at once that Jonathan didn't handle the sails right. He couldn't change them to meet the wind currents.

Nathan noticed it, too, and whispered to Ben. "It's a good thing there isn't much of a breeze."

Ben nodded and whispered to Nathan. "It's a good thing we can swim."

Presently Ben saw black clouds in the southeast. They had formed suddenly, and Ben knew at once what that meant.

"Jonathan!" he cried. "There's a squall coming! Look at those clouds! We must get back!"

"The wind is rising now!" cried Nathan.

Jonathan looked at the clouds and then tried to turn his boat, but he couldn't. The wind blew harder. The sails filled, and the boat raced through the water, *away from land*.

Now it was turning on one side and dipping water. Nathan and Ben had to bail out the boat.

Ben knew they were in real danger. The boat might sink, and they were pretty far from land. He might swim it himself, but the others couldn't. They weren't strong enough.

"Let me take your place, Jonathan," said Ben. "You're tired out."

102

"No," said Jonathan. "I know how to handle this boat."

"Then you'd better tack," said Ben, "and get us back to land."

"You'd better let Ben tack," said Nathan.

"You fellows can't tell me what to do," said Jonathan. "I know."

The clouds became blacker. The wind blew harder. The boat raced faster. It was headed toward the angry ocean.

Suddenly Ben knew what he had to do. No use talking to the pig-headed Jonathan. No use drowning either. He whispered something to Nathan, and Nathan nodded.

Then Ben went up to Jonathan quietly, and hit him with that good, strong Franklin fist.

Jonathan dropped to the deck. Before he could rise, Ben had a rope around his feet. Nathan was tying his hands. In another minute Jonathan was helpless.

Of course he yelled and told them the awful things his father would do to them, but the boys did not care what he said. The wind was now shrieking louder than Jonathan.

Ben worked hard to keep the boat from sinking. He tacked and headed into the wind.

He had heard sailors say this was the right thing to do, but it took courage. It was like a soldier marching toward the enemy guns.

For a time Ben feared he'd never get the boat to land. Jonathan was sure he wouldn't. He was so frightened he was crying.

Nathan was frightened, too, but he thought Ben would save them somehow.

Ben did save them. But it wasn't just somehow! He saved them because he knew how! At last they reached the dock. Three anxious fathers ran to help the boys.

So did several sailors. "That was smart sailing, lad," one told Ben.

"Aye! Aye!" cried others.

They surrounded Ben. They wanted to shake his hand and pat his back.

Mr. Franklin had to push through the crowd to get to Ben. "Thank goodness you're safe!" he cried. "We've been watching you ever since the squall came up. We were afraid for a while——"

"I can't talk now, Father. I have to untie Jonathan," Ben explained.

But Jonathan already had been untied. He had told his father the truth. He had added, "I'm glad Ben hit me."

"So am I," Mr. Bell agreed, "and from now on, Ben is to take full charge of your boat whenever there is trouble."

"Nathan, Ben is always to be the skipper of *Glad*," Mr. Morse said. "Trouble or no trouble, he's your captain."

Ben also became the skipper of the *White Lily*, no matter what kind of weather.

"I want to learn how you manage the sails," Jonathan told him, "and how you tack and everything you know about sailing."

This pleased Ben. It also pleased him to hear Jonathan's, "Aye, aye, Skipper."

Aboard their own craft, the *Glad*, Nathan never forgot to call Ben Skipper.

No matter who said it, Ben loved it. He had made up his mind. He was going to be a real skipper. He'd own a big boat. He'd sail across the ocean. He'd see the world.

"No making candles and soap in a stuffy, smelly room," he declared. But he only said this to himself. It was his secret.

Mrs. Sourface
and Ben

ANGRY MRS. SOURFACE walked down Union Street. It was a narrow, crooked street, and she was afraid she would miss the sign of the Blue Ball. She twisted her long neck first this way, and then that. And the more she twisted, the angrier she grew.

"If I don't find that sign pretty soon," she said to herself, "I'll get the constable, that's what I will. It must be nearby."

"Ah-ha!" Here it was at last. A blue ball about the size of a coconut swung before a small house. Josiah Franklin's name was on the ball. Here was his candle-and-soap shop.

Well, Mrs. Sourface went into the shop just like an angry squall on Boston Bay.

"John!" she screeched. "John!"

John Franklin didn't answer nor come from the back of the shop where she had seen him working.

Instead, came a much younger boy, a handsome round-faced boy about eleven. He wore a big white cap and a leather apron.

"Good morning," he said with a smile.

"Well!" she exclaimed. "What are you doing here, Ben Franklin? Why aren't you in school?"

"I'm the new apprentice here. I'm to learn my father's trade."

"Humph! I reckon the school master put you out. Wouldn't you mind him? Or were you too lazy to get your lessons? It was something bad, I'm thinking.

"It wasn't any of those things, ma'am. Father told the master he needed me. You see, John has left."

"What's that? You say John left? Where did he go?" Mrs. Sourface asked.

"He's gone into business for himself," Ben said. "He has a candle-and-soap shop in Rhode Island now."

"Well, he cheated me, that's what he did! Look at this bar of soap I bought from him last week. I didn't open my bag till this morning, and a big chunk was off that corner."

Ben looked at the soap gravely.

"Could you have had something heavy in your bag that day?" he asked.

"Well, I did have an iron candle-holder, but I'm sure it didn't break the soap. You needn't be making excuses, young man. I'll shake out my bag and show you. There won't be any chunk of soap in it, I promise you."

Mrs. Sourface shook her bag. Out dropped the piece of soap!

"Well! If that doesn't beat all!" she said.

Her face turned very red. "I looked in my bag before I came. I didn't see it."

"Oh, it just stuck in a corner," said Ben. "But it's caused you some trouble, so I'm going to give you an extra bar."

"You are? Why, Ben, that's very handsome of you." And really she smiled!

"Here it is," said Ben. "Father will be glad you came to see about it."

"I'll be coming here the rest of my days, anyway as long as you are here, Ben."

She started out. Then she came back.

"Ben," she said, "I'm really sorry you had to leave school. Everyone said you were learning fast. I knew you weren't put out. I just said it."

"I knew that," said Ben. He smiled at Mrs. Sourface, and Mrs. Sourface smiled at Ben.

The squall was over. The sun was shining again. The winds were quiet.

"I'm sure your parents hated to take you out

of school, Ben. But you'll learn a trade, and that's important, too!"

"Father said I ought to make a good living after I learn his trade."

"Indeed you should! It's a very good business in a city like this. Our winters are always long, and it gets dark early in the late afternoon during the winter."

"So candles must be lighted early," Ben added laughingly.

Mrs. Sourface nodded. Then she went on. "The winter sun comes up late here. The winter mornings are always dark."

"So candles must again be lighted early, and that is good for the candle business, too."

"It certainly keeps people busy buying them," Mrs. Sourface replied, "and soap is needed the year round."

"That's why we make it, ma'am,—large bars, too, with no corners missing."

Mrs. Sourface laughed. "You'll get along. You're smart, Ben. I like smart boys." Then she said goodby and left.

"She nice—I like her," Ben thought. "It's too bad about her name. She isn't sour when you know her."

So, for a time, all was well with the new apprentice at the sign of the Blue Ball.

The customers liked him. His father was pleased with his work. His mother was happy.

"Now Ben will stay at home," she thought. "He'll forget about seeing the world."

Advice from Ben

"ABIAH," SAID Mr. Franklin one night after all the young Franklins were in bed, "I want to talk to you about Ben."

Mrs. Franklin put down her knitting. "Is something wrong?" she asked. "Isn't he doing his work?"

"Oh, his work is well done. The trouble is, he hates it."

"I'm sorry to hear that, Josiah."

"He's been unhappy in the shop for some time. I noticed it, but I thought he was sad because Nathan had moved away from Boston. But I was mistaken. This morning he told me he didn't like the candle business, nor the soap either. He said he hated the very smell of grease."

"Did he say he wanted to leave you?" asked Mrs. Franklin quickly.

"That isn't the fashion nowadays with apprentices. They just disappear in the night."

"I know," said Abiah sadly.

"At least fifteen apprentice boys have run away from Boston this year," Mr. Franklin continued.

"That many!" exclaimed Mrs. Franklin.

"Yes, no one knows whether they went to sea or to the woods. Their fathers and masters have asked dozens of hunters and ship captains about them, too."

"I hope you told Ben about that."

"I did, but it was like pouring water on a duck's back. He said he'd know how to take care of himself if he ran away. That's the trouble, Abiah. Boys of his age think they can do anything."

"They think they are wiser than their parents. Josiah was like that when he was around twelve. He thought it would be wonderful to be a sailor and sail away to faraway lands. He wouldn't listen to you."

"I told him that some ship captains would whip boys if they couldn't do a sailor's work, and that they even sold the boys in foreign lands for slaves. Still he didn't listen."

"Ben is too much like Josiah."

"I hope Ben will become interested in some trade. I took him to several shops this afternoon. We went to a cooper's, a carpenter's, a hatter's, a weaver's, and a tool-maker's."

"Was he interested in at least one."

"He was interested in all. He asked the workers dozens of questions. That's the way he is. He wanted to know about everything, but he doesn't want to be tied down to any one trade. He told me on our way back."

"Not tied down! What did he mean? He knows he has to learn some trade and make his own living." Mrs. Franklin was worried.

"He said he wants to see the world first."

"Did he mean—go to sea?" she asked.

"What else? It's the only way a poor boy can travel," Mr. Franklin answered.

"But he knows we won't consent!"

"He won't ask our consent when he's ready to go," said Mr. Franklin sadly.

"I couldn't bear it if we lost another son," Abiah said. Her voice trembled, and her eyes filled with tears.

"I'll find a way to keep Ben here. I'll have two or three months. The weather is too cold for runaways now."

"They couldn't get to an Indian village. The snow is still deep in the forest, and winds are bitterly cold. The boys would freeze to death if they tried."

118

"Neither can they hide on ships as workers. There are great storms on the ocean now, and no captain wants a seasick boy aboard. He couldn't work, for a time at least."

"I wonder if Ben has thought of these things."

"I'll see to it that he does, Abiah," Mr. Franklin promised his wife.

A SECRET MEETING

Spring had come and gone. Now summer was here, and Ben Franklin was still at home. He was busier than ever in his father's shop.

His brother Peter had gone to Rhode Island to help John in his new shop. There was more work for Thomas and Ben.

Ben was never too busy to make friends. He had met several young apprentices this summer and liked them. He met the boys every evening now in the big Boston park. Thomas met some of his friends there, too. So the two brothers always left home together.

Their father didn't object to their going out. "You boys have been shut up all day in a stuffy room," he said. "You've been breathing candle and soap grease. You should go to the park for fresh air."

"We'll have early suppers," their mother added. "That will give you more time with the friends you may meet there."

"But you must never stay late," Mr. Franklin said firmly. "Evil things have happened in that park at night. Many persons have been robbed and beaten. You must be home by eight o'clock sharp. Don't be late."

Mr. Franklin let Thomas carry his watch. Exactly at half-past seven, Thomas left his friends. He knew that Ben met apprentices near the park tool house. When Thomas reached it, he whistled. Ben came at once.

They were always home by eight, but one night was different. Neither boy knew that it would be when they parted. Each went his own way after they reached the park.

It was a bright moonlight night. Ben clearly saw the bench where he and his friends always met, but there was only one boy there. There usually were five or six boys.

This one boy came to meet him. "I was waiting for you, Ben," he said. "Mike told me to bring you to his house. We're to meet there. His master has gone away for the night."

"I can't go, Simon. I'm afraid I couldn't get back in time to meet my brother."

"You can leave early. The boys are expecting you, Ben. They want your advice," Simon insisted to Ben.

"What about? Is it running away? Do they want me to go with them? Is that it?"

"I don't know," Simon admitted.

"Well, I'm not running away. You can tell the boys that, and I'll go home."

"But Mike said he needed you. He said you knew so much about things, and this was very important. I believe it, too, for he was very excited about something."

"Well, then, I'll go." But Ben was sorry when they reached the dark house. Not a light showed through the front shutters.

"My goodness!" Ben exclaimed. "I'm afraid to go into that place."

"Mike said they'd be in the kitchen."

Ben and Simon went to the back door. It was dark there, too, but Simon knocked three times very softly.

A tall boy of fourteen or so opened the door. "S-sh!" he whispered. "Come in." Then he closed the door quickly and quietly.

"What's the matter, Mike?" Ben asked softly. "Did your master come back?"

"No, thank goodness! But he probably told the constable to watch the house tonight," Mike replied, admitting his fear.

"We didn't see anyone about," Simon said.

"I guess your master would be angry if he knew we were here," a boy suggested.

"He'd whip me every day for a week," Mike replied. "But he won't get a chance. I'll be gone. We'll all be gone, boys." He spoke to the five boys sitting on the floor.

Ben looked at the boys as they nodded their heads. Then he and Simon sat down by them.

The boys were all between twelve and thirteen years old. They were so thin their shoulder blades seemed about to break through their shirts. Their leader, Mike, looked like an old man who had grown old from too hard work.

Ben wished he could help them. "They're all half-starved," he thought, "and they are all worked to death."

Mike stood at the table. "The meeting will begin," he said. "You all must get back early."

"If we don't we will get a good beating," one boy suggestèd.

"And not a bite of food tomorrow," another added quickly.

Just then there was a noise in the hall next to the kitchen. It wasn't a loud noise, but everyone heard it. Everyone was frightened, too.

Some thought their masters had come after them. Mike thought his master hadn't gone away after all. Ben thought of the constable.

A DOUBTFUL BEN

You could have heard a pin drop in that room for a while. But no master opened the door. Neither did a constable come.

"I guess it was just the old house creaking," Mike suggested. "The stairs always creak like that when I try to creep down or up."

The boys laughed. They knew all about that.

"Of course you hated to wake your master," Ben joked.

The others laughed again. Every one of them, except Ben and Mike, had crept down creaky stairs that evening. They weren't allowed to leave after supper, and woe to them if their masters caught them.

Then Mike asked Ben to come to the table. "We want your advice," he said.

Ben went to the front. "What's the trouble?" Ben asked.

"We've decided to run away. We can't stand it any longer. We can't work from daylight till night on nothing but thin soup and a little sour bread," Mike explained.

"Of course you can't," Ben replied. "I don't blame you for leaving, but don't go to the Indians. Brown Beaver told Father the chief didn't want runaway boys. It made trouble for him with white men."

"No Indians for us. We're going to a foreign land. A ship's captain offered to take us."

"How did that happen, Mike?" Ben asked.

"Well, this morning I went to the dock with my master. He was going to New York. I carried his bag aboard his ship.

"When I went back, a sailor stopped me on the dock. He said he wanted to speak to me. He took me to one side away from everyone. He said the captain of his ship felt sorry for apprentices and wanted to help them. He asked if I knew any boys who wanted to run away."

"Did you tell him about us?" Simon asked quickly and eagerly.

"I did. I said I was going to tell you. He told me to bring you boys down to the ship tonight. He said the captain would hide us until they sailed at dawn."

"Then what?" Ben asked.

"Then he'd take us to another country."

"It's against the law to help runaways. That captain could be put in jail."

"The sailor spoke of that, Ben, but he said the captain was kind-hearted. He was willing to take the risk."

"It all sounds fishy to me," Ben declared.

"No, no! I'm sure he told the truth. He said we'd have all the food we could eat, and we wouldn't have to work unless we wanted to."

"Food!" a boy cried. "I say we go!"

"Let's go! Let's go!" others cried and jumped to their feet.

"Sit down!" Mike ordered. "We haven't heard Ben's advice yet."

"I can't give any until I have more facts. First, where was this ship going, Mike?"

"The sailor said to some foreign country."

"That sounds bad to me. Another thing I'd like to know. Did he tell you the ship's name?"

"No, when I asked him, he said he'd put us aboard. He'd wait for us on the dock. I told him we'd be there, and then I left."

128

"You left—without knowing the ship's name?"

"I got to thinking about that, Ben. So I went back right away. I hid behind freight and watched the sailor. When he started to the ships, I followed him. I saw him go aboard one. I saw her name—the *Mary Ann*."

"Good! Now we have something to go on. I'll ask my brother-in-law about this ship and the captain himself. I've told you about him. His name is Holmes."

"Yes, I remember," Mike replied. "But you mustn't tell him, Ben. The sailor said we mustn't tell anyone."

"I don't care what he said. Why didn't he tell you where you were going?"

"I guess he forgot that."

"Forgot nothing! He was lying to you, Mike. If he'd been honest, he'd have told you that the first thing. Did he say what you would do after you got there?"

"No—he didn't."

"Don't go, Mike! Don't go, boys! You wouldn't catch me running away unless I knew where I was going, and what I'd have to do."

"But it's such a good chance to get away," Mike said. "We might never have another."

"You might be jumping from the frying pan into the fire, too. I know your masters are mean, but others might be worse."

The boys didn't know what to think. Mike himself was puzzled. They just looked at Ben.

Now there was a noise at the door to the hall. Eight scared boys saw the knob turning. Then the door opened.

THE CONSTABLES

Two young men entered the room. They wore the uniform of the Boston deputy constables. They spoke kindly to the frightened boys.

"We were sent here to watch the house," one explained. "We were to enter if anyone besides Mike came into the house. We heard your secret, boys. We listened at the door."

"And you're not sailing on the *Mary Ann*," the other deputy told them. "You're all going down to the chief constable's office. But you'll not be punished," he added quickly. "You haven't done anything wrong. You just talked about running away."

"Do I have to go?" Ben asked. "I ought to get home. I wasn't planning to run away."

"What's your name?" one deputy asked.

"Ben Franklin," was the prompt reply.

"Oh, you're the boy who gave the good advice. Sorry, but you must come with us, Ben. We were ordered to bring everyone. Get your hats, boys, and come along."

Eight boys were marched to the chief constable's office. A third deputy watched them

131

while they waited in the hall. The other two went into the chief's office.

After a long time they came out. Both seemed pleased about something.

"You won't have to stay much longer," one said. "The chief might want Mike to tell his story, but maybe not. We've already told him. He was very glad to get the ship's name.

"Indeed he was," the other deputy added. "He sent a dozen deputies to board the *Mary Ann* at once. They were to arrest that captain and sailor."

"Did they get them?" Ben asked.

"They did. The rascals are in the office now. The chief has laid down the law to them. They're scared to death. The captain has confessed what he meant to do with you boys. He was going to sell you to foreign masters."

"Sell us!" exclaimed Mike. "Do you mean— like—like slaves?"

"Exactly. That's what he did with those fifteen boys who disappeared. The sailor got his share of the money."

"They'll both spend the rest of their lives in prison," the other added. "They're both real scoundrels. After this you'd better listen to that boy who gave you such good advice. I don't remember his name."

"Ben Franklin!" the boys shouted.

"Stand up, Ben," the man said.

Ben stood. The man went on. "You have a lot of common sense, lad. It's a pleasure to know there's a boy like you."

"Thanks, sir, thanks," Ben replied.

Now the other deputy spoke. "Well, the chief hasn't sent for you, so you may leave. But first you're to go to an eating place with us. The chief said you were to have a good supper—all you can eat. Come along."

Seven grateful apprentices gladly went with

the deputies. Ben hurried on to meet his brother Thomas in the park.

Only one master ever knew the truth about that night. He was Josiah Franklin. Ben told his father as soon as he reached home.

"I'm glad you weren't running away, Ben," Mr. Franklin told his young son.

"I never will, Father—not unless I have a mean master," Ben promised.

"You will never have that, Son, not while I live anyway."

A Trade for Ben

JAMES FRANKLIN had come back from London. He had been a printer's apprentice there for a long time. He now owned a print shop in Boston, and his business was growing rapidly.

"I need an apprentice," he told his father one day. "I want a smart, likely lad who can read anything."

"What would you say to Ben?" asked Mr. Franklin. "He is smart and likely, and he can read anything."

"Does he want to learn the printer's trade?" asked James. "If he does, I'll be glad to have him for a helper."

But, alas, Ben did not want to learn the printer's trade. "I want to travel," he said. "I want to be a sailor and go around the world."

"You can do that when you are older," said his father. "Just now it will be best for you to go with your brother."

"How long would I have to stay with him?" Ben asked.

"The law says an apprentice must stay with his master until he is twenty-one years old."

"But I'm only twelve years old! That will be nine years!"

"It will take that long to learn the printing business, Ben."

"Oh, I just can't do it, Father. I'm sorry, Mother. I'd like to please you, but I can't bear to think of it. Nine years working with type! I would hate it."

Then his mother cried, and there were tears in his father's eyes.

Ben couldn't stand that for he loved his parents dearly. So at last he consented.

Then James brought a paper for Ben to sign. It was called an Agreement, and James had to sign it, too.

This Agreement declared that James Franklin must teach Ben Franklin the printer's trade and must board and clothe him, with no wages paid. It declared, also, that Ben Franklin must obey James Franklin in all things.

This paper was signed by Mr. Josiah Franklin, too, to show he gave his consent.

So now James was Ben's "master," and Ben was a "printer's boy."

The Franklin family hated to see Ben leave home with his little chest of clothing. But that's the way things were done in Boston at that time.

They were thankful for one thing, however: "Now Ben can't go to sea," they said. "Now he is bound to James by the law."

Ben learned fast. He was soon setting type and doing it well and rapidly. He liked the work, too. He liked it better and better every day.

James noticed that Ben planned his work before he began. He sorted the type, and placed each kind in its own case so each font, or type of one size or style, was always complete. There was no time lost hunting for this or that letter.

Neither was any time lost asking James how to spell words. Ben was a good speller.

He was polite to the customers. He would go to any trouble to help them write the notices they wanted printed. He ran errands and wheeled printing paper through the streets.

James sent Ben to the finest homes with work. He knew that Ben would never be rude or ask foolish questions. Indeed, Ben never talked much. He had formed the habit of listening in his father's home.

Once he delivered a printed sermon at the home of a famous preacher, Cotton Mather. Mr. Mather had him come to his library, and Ben saw a sight he had never seen before. Great bookcases reached from ceiling to floor, all of them filled with books.

The boy was delighted. "Oh, if I could only reading in such a beautiful place!" he said to himself. "If I could only own books like these! But of course I can't. That is only for the rich and the great."

He didn't dream that he, poor Ben Franklin, a "printer's boy," was to have, one day, a large library of his own. Great bookcases were to be filled with books.

READING BOOKS

Ben had long working hours, from daylight until dark. But every night, no matter how tired he was, he read the books that James had brought from London.

There were only a few, so before long he was looking for more books to read. Where could he get them? No one he knew owned books.

Then he had some good luck. He had become friendly with John Collins, who was an apprentice in a bookseller's shop. Ben had told John how he longed for books to read.

John had told his master, and the master had offered to lend Ben new books from his store. But each book had to be returned early the next morning, as clean and fresh as a new book should be.

So Ben read late at night. A few times he read all night in order to return the book on time. Not once did he fail in this, and the book was always as good as new.

Ben knew he couldn't keep this up. He would be too sleepy to do his work. He must find a way

to buy books. Then he would read when he could. But how could he buy books? He had no money, and he wouldn't have until he was twenty-one. Apprentices received no cash wages—just room, board, and clothing.

At last he thought of a plan. He told James that he would buy his own dinner if James would give him half the money Ben's dinner cost. James agreed at once. It was a good bargain for him. If Ben didn't want to eat roast beef he was foolish, but he could eat what he pleased.

From then on Ben just about starved himself. For his dinner he would eat a thin slice of bread, or a cracker, or a few raisins.

Not another boy in Boston could have stood this, but Ben was strong. He was so strong he could carry a font of type with one hand. Other printers had to use both hands and even then it seemed heavy.

So, because he was strong, and because he

drank plenty of water, he got along for a time. He saved half of the sum James gave him and bought books.

They were paper-backed books about almost everything in the world—reindeer, stars, ink, rice, swamps, sponges, pearls, and camels.

Ben could read at noon now, for his little dinner was over in five minutes. For an hour he traveled in faraway lands. He saw strange people and cities. He floated down wide rivers and climbed high mountains. He rode camels and drove reindeer.

How he did enjoy it! He didn't even think of going to sea any more.

PATTERNS AND ARITHMETIC

One day an old lady came to the print shop, a Mrs. Snow. She wanted strips of linen printed for curtains.

James had advertised that he was ready to print calico or linen in three colors, red, yellow, and blue.

Mrs. Snow selected a pattern, and then gave Ben the order. She said, "My curtains are three yards long and one yard wide. I want the pattern printed in red all the way around. There are four curtains. Now, how many yards of pattern will that make, and what will it cost?"

Poor Ben! He figured, and he figured, but he couldn't work it. He had to ask James.

James didn't like this. He said sharply, "You're supposed to do your own work."

That very night Ben bought an arithmetic and began to teach himself. He got up very early and studied. He studied at noon. He sat up late at night and studied. Before long he understood figuring, and then it was easy for him.

One day Miss Dolly Shippen came to the shop. "Ben," she said, "I want a calico skirt printed with your yellow pattern. The skirt is seven and one-half yards wide, and I want the pattern repeated three times. What will it cost, please?"

In just about two minutes Ben told her. He didn't have to go to James that time, nor ever again. Indeed, he did the figuring for all the orders after that.

James certainly had the "smart, likely lad" for whom he had been looking.

The Great Secret

JAMES FRANKLIN was planning to print a news-paper. There was already one in Boston, but James thought there could be one more.

His friends told him he was making a mistake. One man said one paper was enough for all America. But two friends said they would write pieces for it, if James was determined to print it.

James was determined! So the pieces were written. The paper was printed, and Ben sold it on the streets.

It was called the *New England Courant,* and sold well from the start.

The writers were delighted. They said everyone was praising their pieces. They told what this one said, and what that one said, and how happy it made them to make others so happy.

Ben was setting type in the next room, but he couldn't help hearing this talk. It put a new idea into his head.

Why shouldn't he write for the *Courant*, too? He was sixteen now, and he had been writing pieces secretly for some time.

No one knew this except his friend John Collins. Now he told John about his new idea.

"You can write well enough," said John, "but will your brother print it?"

"I'm afraid he won't," said Ben. "He wants well-known persons so the paper will sell better."

"Couldn't you persuade him, Ben?"

"I'm sure I couldn't, but I'll write the piece anyway," said Ben. "I'll write something that will make people laugh. I'll make fun of things that should be made fun of."

"That's the idea!" said John.

"I'll give them a rub about these mudholes in the streets," Ben chuckled.

"That's great, Ben, just great."

SILENCE DOGOOD

For several nights, up in a tiny attic room, candles burned till very late. They lighted up the face of a happy boy who was writing his "piece." Now and then he would stop to laugh.

"This is funny," he would say to himself.

He pretended he was a widow, a "Mrs. Silence Dogood." He made her a silly, empty-headed kind of woman, who was always saying and doing foolish things. It was really a "comic strip," only it was in writing, instead of drawings.

Ben had decided to keep it a secret. He was certain James would not print it, if he knew Ben had written it.

So he changed his handwriting when he copied the story, and he signed it "Silence Dogood."

He wanted to put it under the print-shop door that very night. But could he get out of the house without James seeing him? Could he even get out of his room without being heard?

He'd take off his shoes and carry them. But his door! Suppose it should squeak! It did sometimes, but it must not tonight!

He turned the knob slowly and gently. He opened that door so quietly a fly wouldn't have noticed it.

He was now in a dark hall. He didn't dare to carry a lighted candle for fear he would be seen. He had to go down two flights of stairs in the dark. One stumble, and out would come Master James from his bedroom.

So down, down, he crept, as softly as a cat. He reached the street door and opened it without making a sound.

He put on his shoes and ran all the way to James's printing house in Queen Street.

Quickly he put his envelope under the door! It was done! What would happen next? Would James guess who wrote it?

Then he crept back into the house. He went up the dark stairs, through the dark hall, and into his own room. No one had seen him. He had been lucky so far.

THE ENVELOPE

The next morning a large envelope was found under the print-shop door. And who should find it but Ben! Wasn't that strange?

He *happened* to be the first one in the shop that morning. Wasn't that strange, too?

When James came, Ben gave him the envelope. "It was under the door," he said.

"I wonder if it's something the writer is

ashamed of," said James. "It must be, or he wouldn't come like a thief in the night."

All this time he was opening the envelope. Now he began to read the papers. Ben went back to sorting type into its case, but he kept one eye on James.

Would James know his handwriting? Would James print it if he knew? Would James think the piece was funny?

That was a bad three minutes for Ben. But what was this? James was smiling! Now he was actually laughing!

Just then some of the writers for the *Courant* came in the shop. And James Franklin read Ben's piece out loud!

The writers laughed and laughed, and James laughed with them. They stopped for a moment, and then they all laughed again.

"That's real wit," Ben heard one say.

"It will make everyone laugh," said another.

"It's the funniest thing ever written in this town," said the third.

Ben's heart was pounding, he was so excited. But he was to hear more.

"I'd give a pretty penny to know who wrote it," said James. "Have you any idea who this 'Silence Dogood' can be?"

"It must be one of our Boston wits," said one.

"It might be a professor in Harvard College," said another.

So they went on guessing and guessing. And every person they named was some well-known man in Boston!

The piece was printed in the *Courant*. When Ben saw *his* piece, actually *in print,* he wanted to shout, he was so happy.

John Collins did shout, he was so happy. His young friend, only sixteen, was a writer!

Both boys kept the great secret, and no one even guessed the truth.

Before long the whole town was laughing about Silence Dogood and her foolish talk. Ben had her ask if the mudholes in the Boston streets were made there on purpose.

"If so, it was truly a real kindness to animals," she said.

"Mrs. Mack can bring her twenty pigs here to wallow. No use to take them to the creek— such a long trip for them. Of course their grunting may disturb some folks, but surely not lovers of good bacon."

"And were grunts any worse than croaks?" she asked. "The holes were full of frogs, hundreds of them. They kept up a terrible din all night long and scared little children into fits.

"The mud is nice for flies and mosquitoes, too," she said. "There is the mud to breed in, and the people to light on, all close together. Very handy indeed!"

154

Then she told how she fell into one of these holes in her Sunday clothes. When she got out, she found a frog in each pocket and tadpoles in her shoes.

And that wasn't all—the constable arrested her for swimming on Sunday.

The papers sold like hot cakes. Everyone wanted to read the story about Silence Dogood and the mudholes.

Ben had to run back to the print shop for more a dozen times that day.

James was delighted. He told Ben, "I don't think anyone in Boston really liked mudholes in the streets."

But James was wrong. The next day a woman came to the shop. James was in his office. He was talking to one of his writers.

"Which one of you is the owner of this news-paper?" she asked sharply.

"I am, ma'am," James replied. "What can I do

for you? Won't you sit down?" He motioned to a chair nearby.

"No, I won't sit down," she said angrily. "How dare you talk about me the way you did?"

"Lady, lady, wait a minute! I didn't talk about you. I don't even know you."

"You've turned folks against me. You have everyone laughing about me and my pigs."

"Oh! You mean that piece in the *Courant* yesterday—about the mudholes?"

"I do. I'll have you up before the judge. That's what I will."

"But I didn't write it, ma'am."

"Then who did?"

The young printer's apprentice in the next room wasn't working now. He was listening to hear his brother's answer.

"Lady, I'm sorry, but I can't tell you," James said. "I don't know myself. It was put under the door here one night."

"Humph! That's a likely story."

"It's true, ma'am," the writer put in. "I was here when he opened the envelope."

"Well, anyway, you printed it," she told James. "I want you to know I have a right to let my pigs wallow in the mudholes."

"Oh! So that's the trouble. So you're the owner of those pigs?"

"I am, sir. That's the way I make my living."

"Wouldn't it be better to move into the country and raise your pigs there?" James asked.

"Do you want me scalped by Indians?"

"Do you think a city is safer?"

"Of course it is. Indians wouldn't dare attack anyone here. There are many people about who wouldn't let anything happen to me."

"Then why don't you do something for them?"

"What do you mean?"

"Well, they certainly can't enjoy the smell of your pigsty. I know I wouldn't."

"That's another thing I have against you. They've never complained about the pigs till after they read your paper. They told me I had no business to have pigs in a city."

"Hurrah!" Ben said to himself.

"Your neighbors were right," James said firmly.

"What do you expect me to do—starve?"

"Sell your pigs, ma'am, and find something else to do," James suggested politely.

"Something that smells sweeter," the writer added. "You'd better take Mr. Franklin's advice. Those mudholes will be filled soon."

"I'll see about that. I'll go to the Governor, that's what I'll do. I'll make you pay for this, James Franklin. It's all your fault. Silence Dogood, indeed!"

Then she left, but she banged the door good and hard after her.

"Well! Well!" James exclaimed.

"That's what I say," the writer agreed.

"One just can't please everybody," James said. "I wonder what will happen next."

A lot of people wondered. They had stopped laughing now and had begun to think. They remembered what Silence Dogood had said about pigs, flies, and mosquitoes.

Then they wrote letters to the Governor. They told him that pigs were driving people from the streets and that the flies and mosquitoes the pigs brought were driving people from their homes.

"Must we leave Boston?" the people asked. "Must we find a better place to live?"

In a short time every mudhole was filled.

"Hurray for Silence Dogood!" John cried.

"She really did good, didn't she?" Ben asked.

"She did, thanks to you. She's made Boston a better place in which to live."

"That makes me happy."

"Oh, do you know what that woman did with her pigs?" John asked.

"She sold them. Now she's making bread to sell. Her neighbors buy it, too."

"So things have turned out well for everyone."

"For everyone except me. James won't want any more pieces about Silence. He's had so much trouble over this one."

"We'll wait and see, Ben."

"That's all we can do, John, wait and see."

BEN'S SECOND PIECE

It wasn't long until James Franklin put a certain notice in the *Courant*. He asked "Silence Dogood" to send another such piece to him. The author could bring it to the office of the *Courant*, and no questions would be asked. Or he could take it to the Sign of the Blue Ball in Union Street, and no questions would be asked.

"I can write another piece," Ben told John Collins. "There are plenty of things in Boston that should be made fun of. There's the way they punish people by putting them in the stocks."

Stocks were a large heavy frame with holes for arms and legs. The sinner sat behind the frame. His legs, or arms, or both, were thrust through the holes and held there by locks.

Sometimes he would be kept there all day or longer and in all kinds of weather.

These stocks were always in an open place, where everyone could see the poor man and perhaps make fun of him.

"It's downright cruel," said John. "I've hated it for years."

"They punish people for such little things," said Ben, "like taking a walk or a swim on Sunday—or for talking against the high taxes."

"Or for saying your neighbor is lazy," said John. "Or for saying he doesn't tell the truth."

"I'll have Silence Dogood make fun of the stocks," said Ben.

"Be careful," John warned, "or you'll find your arms in those holes some day."

"I don't care," said Ben. "I'll do it anyway."

Again candles burned late at night in the attic room. Again they lighted up the face of a happy boy who was writing his second piece. Again he laughed as he wrote, and again he said out loud, "This is really funny."

At last it was finished, copied, and signed "Silence Dogood." But it was not taken either to the *Courant* or to the Blue Ball in Union Street. It was put under the door of the printing house in Queen Street. Ben was taking no chances on brother James.

THE HOLES IN THE STOCKS AND THE SOCKS

"Ha, ha!" laughed the readers of the *Courant*. "Here is Silence Dogood again! And if she hasn't her six children with her!"

162

She had indeed. The widow and children were out, dressed in their Sunday clothes. On Milk Street they met Mrs. Goodheart.

"Oh, my dear," said Silence, "I guess you know where we've been."

"No," said Mrs. Goodheart, "I don't."

"Why, to the stocks of course, to see poor Bill Fiddlesticks. He's been in the frame since sunup. Haven't you seen him?"

"I couldn't go," said Mrs. Goodheart. But to herself she said, "I wouldn't go"

"I wouldn't have missed it for anything," said the Widow Dogood. "It was like a Christmas tree. The children will never forget it."

"No," said Mrs. Goodheart to herself, "they never will, the poor things."

"You'd never guess what happened," Silence went on. "Bill's feet were so big they wouldn't go through the holes in the stocks, and they had to take off his shoes. Ha, ha, ha, ha!"

Mrs. Goodheart didn't even smile. "The constable should have opened the frame," she said. "The holes are made small so they can't pull their feet out."

"Oh, my dear! You really couldn't expect that," said Silence. "The frame is heavy to lift."

"I see," said Mrs. Goodheart. "It would be too bad to make the constable go to any extra trouble, I suppose."

"I'm glad he didn't," said Mrs. Dogood. "We wouldn't have had all that fun. Ha, ha, ha!"

"Ha, ha, ha!" laughed the children.

"Tell the lady what you saw, dears."

"Holes in his socks!" yelled the children.

"You mean holes in the stocks," Mrs. Goodheart corrected them.

"No, no!" cried Silence. "Not holes in the stocks! Holes in his socks, Bill's socks! You should have heard the people laugh. He'll never live that down."

"Will he live down his crime?" asked Mrs. Goodheart sadly.

"Crime? What crime?" said Silence.

"Don't you know why Bill was there?"

"Oh, I never pay any attention to that. Well, good-by, my dear. Come on, children. Haven't we had a good time?"

Everyone laughed at this story at first. Then some began to think. Was it right to laugh at a man being punished? Should anyone think it funny to see a man suffer from cramped legs and arms—from sun, winds, or rains?

The people of Boston talked about this until even the Governor had to listen. It took a long time, but Boston finally burned her stocks.

NO LONGER A SECRET

People kept on asking for more "Dogood Stories." James Franklin kept on advertising

165

for them, and Ben Franklin kept on writing them. He hadn't gone about Boston with his eyes shut, and he always knew something that would make a funny story.

Now he decided to write about the way cruel masters treated their young apprentices.

He had Silence Dogood praise these masters. "They know how to make those lazy boys work," she told her children.

"The boys are awfully skinny," her oldest boy said.

"It's their own fault. They won't eat what their masters give them. A rich master told me that himself."

"Well—yes, that's what I've heard people say."

"I want to be a rich master sometime."

"I hope you will. You won't have to pay your apprentices anything. You can work them all day long. You shouldn't give them much food. They couldn't work if they were stuffed."

Ben heard James read this story aloud to a writer. "I can't print this," he said, "I'd make too many enemies. Besides, I don't know whether it is true."

Then Ben lost his head. He went into the office and faced his astonished brother. "It is true!" he cried. "Every word of it is the truth, I know."

"How would you know?" James asked.

"I knew several apprentices. I belonged to their club. I knew what I was doing when I wrote that piece."

"When you what——?"

"I didn't mean to tell you. It just slipped out. I wrote the Silence Dogwood stories."

James was flabbergasted. "You wrote those stories! You couldn't! I don't believe it!"

Ben showed his first papers, before he had copied them. James looked them over carefully. At last he had to believe it.

James told his friends who also were flabbergasted. They refused to believe it at first. "What! That printer boy? It's impossible!"

James showed them Ben's first papers, and then they had to believe it. They made a great fuss oven Ben and praised him so much James was a little jealous.

Before long everyone in Boston knew who wrote the "Dogood Stories." Everyone said there wasn't another boy like Ben Franklin in all America. That also made James a little jealous.

Mr. and Mrs. Franklin were very proud of Ben.

"I'm so glad he likes to write," said Mrs. Franklin. "That will keep him in Boston."

"Yes," said Mr. Franklin, "there's no danger of Ben running away now."

The Quarrels

A CHANGE HAD come over James Franklin. He had always been kind and lively, but now he was cross and glum.

Ben couldn't understand it. The business was growing, and there were two new apprentices. But nothing pleased James. He found fault with Ben. He scolded him before the other boys. He blamed him for everything that went wrong.

The truth was, James was now very jealous of his younger brother. It made him angry when people praised Ben.

"It is going to the boy's head," he told his father. "He is even saucy to me, his master."

No doubt that was true. Ben had been told so often that he was the smartest boy in Boston. Perhaps it had gone to his head.

Things went from bad to worse, and one day James struck Ben.

This made Ben angry, and he talked back.

Now no apprentice, in Boston, or anywhere else, would dare to talk back, no matter what his master said or did. So of course James was furious and went to his father again.

Mr. Franklin told James to be kinder to Ben. "A little praise won't hurt him," he said.

"You always take Ben's part," said James. Then he treated Ben worse than ever. He even beat him for mistakes the other boys made.

Ben was very unhappy. He told his father that James treated him as if he were a slave, instead of a brother.

Again Josiah Franklin talked to James, but James said, "You're always taking Ben's part."

Down in his heart James Franklin knew that Ben was the best apprentice in the world. But he wouldn't say so. He kept on scolding and beating him.

At last Ben made up his mind to leave James. He would run away from Boston!

THE RUNAWAY

But Ben was not going to sea. He liked the printing business, and he knew the trade from start to finish. He was going to be a printer somewhere, he had decided.

He would go to New York first. If he couldn't get into a print shop there, he would go on to Philadelphia.

He told John Collins his plans, and John promised to help him get away. Ben didn't dare to make the arrangements himself.

John sold Ben's books to raise his passage

money. Then he went to see the captain of a sloop that was sailing for New York that night.

He told the captain that a certain young man was obliged to go to New York on secret business. He was willing to pay something extra if no questions were asked.

The captain agreed and promised to wait for this important passenger. "He might be a little late," John said.

In the meantime Ben had packed his clothing and was waiting for a chance to get his chest out of the house.

He knew that James was going out to see an Indian Dance. These Indians had just come to Boston, and everyone wanted to see them. There would be a great crowd in the park.

The streets would be almost empty, and he hoped to get away without being seen.

So Ben waited up in his room, and John waited down in the street.

Would James never go? What was keeping him? Maybe he had changed his mind and wouldn't go after all. Would Ben have to wait till James had gone to bed? Would the captain wait that long for him?

There were plenty of worries for Ben that night. He hated to leave his parents without even a good-by. But if he told them, they would feel duty-bound to tell James. And James could have him brought back.

Just then he heard James leaving the house. A shrill whistle from below showed that John had seen him go.

Ben then took his chest down, and John helped him carry it through the dark streets to the dock.

The sloop was waiting. The extra passage money was paid. The captain asked no questions, and Ben and his chest were soon aboard.

There was a good breeze, so the little ship sailed at once.

Ben Franklin, only seventeen years old, was leaving his boyhood home. He was sailing toward a new life, in a strange city, among strange people. He had only a little money in his pocket, a dollar or two.

But he had a fortune in his head. *He knew his trade.* He was a good "printer's boy."

THE SEARCH FOR BEN

Another boy had run away from Boston. Another bitter lad was facing danger somewhere.

James talked to John Collins, but John didn't seem to know anything about Ben's plans. Mr. Josiah Franklin went to the docks and talked to captains and sailors, but no one had seen Ben.

Of course Captain Holmes was looking for him all the time. He was Ben's brother-in-law. He owned a sloop that traded in New York and Philadelphia. He tried to find Ben in these cities. He went to a printer's shop in New York and asked about Ben.

Yes, the boy had been there, the printer said, but he couldn't give the boy any work. The New York printer had advised the lad to go to Philadelphia. He had been told there was a printer there who needed help. Ben had said that he would go to Philadelphia.

Of course the printer did not know the boy didn't have enough money for this trip. The printer did not know to tell Captain Holmes that Ben had walked part of the way.

In Philadelphia Captain Holmes heard some talk about a strange lad who had lately come from Boston. They said he landed one day without a cent, and the next day had work in a print shop. They said he could lift a font with one hand.

Captain Holmes was sure they were talking about Ben so he went to this print shop at once.

There was Ben! And he was well and happy! The captain begged him to go back home, but Ben refused. He loved Philadelphia, he said, and he was not going back to Boston to be beaten again by James.

The next week Ben received a letter. It was addressed to:

Benjamin Franklin
Printer's Boy
Philadelphia
Pennsylvania

Care of Keimer's Print Shop

The letter was from his father and Ben was delighted. But Josiah made a mistake when he wrote "Printer's Boy" on the envelope.

Ben was no longer an apprentice with a master over him. He was making good wages.

He had bought good clothing and a watch. He was buying books. He was making friends of young men who also loved books.

Ben wrote a long letter to his father and told him all these things. And he didn't forget to mention his watch, for that was something no apprentice ever owned.

He said James might get a constable to take

him back, but no constable could keep him in Queen Street—not so long as there were dark nights and sailing sloops in the harbor.

Then Josiah Franklin went to Queen Street. "James," he said, "let Ben alone. If you bring him back, he will only run away again. Ben has to be his own master and do his own thinking. He has that kind of mind, and nothing will ever change him."

This time James listened to his father. Soon after, in the *Courant* was this notice:

"James Franklin, Printer in Queen Street, wants a smart, likely lad for an apprentice."

His first smart, likely apprentice was now safe in the city he loved, safe and free.

Ben was free to begin thinking of those wonderful things that were to come out of his wonderful head and astonish the whole world.

Ben's Wonderful Inventions

BENJAMIN FRANKLIN worked hard and prospered in his occupation as a printer. His active mind observed the people around him and created interesting material for putting in the books and newspapers.

Ben remembered and quoted the sayings of his father's guests at the Blue Ball. He put many of these sayings into his famous book *Poor Richard's Almanac*.

Ben wrote his first *Almanac* in 1732 when he was twenty-six years old. People enjoyed reading it so much that Ben published a new one each year for twenty-five years.

179

Ben in a few years had become the owner of the best printing shop in Philadelphia. He had married Deborah Read, one of his first acquaintances in Philadelphia. Together Deborah and Ben worked to build a good business and a very happy home.

As Benjamin Franklin prospered, he gave generously of his money to help Philiadelphia.

He started the first public library, the first fire company, the first paved streets, and dozens of other things—all of them to help people live better. He gave a fortune for free schools for poor children, too.

He was not only generous to the people of Philadelphia, but he was also generous to his relatives in Boston. He went often to see them. He gave them money and presents.

He helped his brother James, for the two brothers had made up and were now good friends.

Mr. Franklin was a very busy man. He was not only a printer. He was an inventor.

He invented a stove. An article appeared in a newspaper of the day: "Mr. Benjamin Franklin has invented a stove. It is the first stove in all the world that will work. This is the greatest gift to the human race. No longer shall our faces burn and our backs freeze at the fireplaces. Thanks to you, Mr. Franklin. Thanks from the human race."

The news of other inventions brought different attitudes in the newspapers.

"Mr. Benjamin Franklin has invented a rocking chair! Shame on you, Ben! Almost all persons are lazy enough now. A chair that rocks will ruin the rest of us. This is not a gift to mankind, dear sir."

"Mr. Benjamin Franklin has invented double spectacles for both near-sighted and far-sighted people. Blessings on your head, Mr. Franklin!"

Mr. Franklin was a real scientist. He tried out something that no man in the world had ever dared do. He had thought of a way to discover what lightning was.

For a long time Mr. Franklin had been wondering about lightning. What was it? Could it be brought out of the clouds down to earth?

At that time no one knew these things. People were terribly afraid of lightning. They thought God was angry at them, and the flashes of fire were flashes of His anger.

Mr. Franklin didn't believe this. He thought lightning was merely electric fire, and he proposed to bring it down to earth with his kite and prove it.

He made a cross of two light strips of wood and fastened a large silk handkerchief to the four ends. To the top of the upright stick, he fastened a sharp-pointed wire, rising a foot or more above the wood.

The kite had a tail, loop, and string just like other kites.

The string was cotton twine. To the end of the twine was tied a silk ribbon which he would hold in his hand.

Where the twine and silk ribbon joined was tied a metal key.

Mr. Franklin believed the pointed wire would draw electric fire from the clouds. He thought this fire would run down to the metal key as soon as the kite and twine were wet. If he were right, he would get a strong shock when he touched the key.

The silk ribbon must be kept dry all the time, or he might get a shock that would kill him. He was taking a great risk, even with the ribbon dry. But he was determined to try the experiment.

The kite was now ready. He had only to wait for the lightning.

One day it came. The sky was black with

thunderclouds when Mr. Franklin went out into a field with his kite. He stood under a shed to keep the silk ribbon dry, and he was careful that the twine did not touch the door frame. He wanted the current to flow freely to the key—it must not be stopped in any way.

Now the black clouds were right over the kite. If it were to happen, it must happen now, as soon as the lightning flashed again, and the rain fell.

The thunder roared! The lightning flashed! Then came the rain.

Mr. Franklin touched the key with his knuckles. At once he received a strong shock, and the key gave off sparks of electric fire.

He was delighted. Again and again he touched the key, and each time he felt the shock and saw the sparks.

He had proved his idea! He had brought this electric fire out of the clouds down to the earth! June 15, 1752, was an exciting day!

Before long every newspaper in America and Europe told their readers about this experiment. They said it was astonishing—one of the most wonderful things any man had ever done.

They said Mr. Benjamin Franklin was a great scientist—one of the greatest in all the world. He had added scientist to his list of achievements— as a printer, author, humorist, and inventor.

Welcome Home

MANY YEARS passed. Then one day a great crowd gathered at a dock in Philadelphia. The people were all gazing at a ship about to land.

Suddenly a man cried out, "There he is! There's Ben Franklin—on the deck there, waving his hand!"

Cannons boomed! Bells rang! People cheered! Men threw their hats into the air! Women waved their handerchiefs!

Benjamin Franklin had come back from France! Benjamin Franklin, the best-loved citizen in America! Benjamin Franklin, almost as great as George Washington!

Between the roar of cannons and the ringing bells, you could hear the people on the dock talking of this great man.

"He has been in France on important business for this country."

"He has been there for years. Congress wouldn't let him come back till now."

"Of course not. America needed a good business man over there. And who was better than Benjamin Franklin?"

"No one! No one in all this country!"

"But he had to be away from his home and family all this time!"

"He said it was his duty to his country."

"Not another man in America would have given up his home for so long a time."

"Except George Washington."

"Yes, of course. They are much alike. If they can do anything for America, they never think of themselves."

"Ben Franklin is a great patriot."

"He's a great man. Just think, he came here a poor boy, a printer. And now look at this crowd, will you! Everyone in Philadelphia is here to welcome him."

"Franklin is a rich man now, but he has worked hard for his money. Four years after he came, he had his own print shop."

"His wife helped him. She took care of the shop while he set up type. They lived back of the shop, too."

"Well, they live in a fine house now. I've heard they have silver and china and more than a thousand books."

"It's true. And his wife wears a scarlet satin cape to church. He sent it to her from France. They say that he sent her presents every time a ship sailed."

"He sent presents to his folks, too, even James. He bought a print shop for James's son."

"He has spent his life trying to help others. No wonder he is the best-loved citizen in the United States of America."

"They love him in France, too. Peddlers sell little statues of him on the streets."

"The Queen of France sent her own carriage to him for a trip."

"Great scholars all over Europe wanted to hear him talk about science."

"Great inventors all over the world wanted his advice about their inventions."

"Great English doctors wanted to hear about his discovery of air germs."

"No wonder Americans are proud of him! There isn't a man like him in all the world—a man who knows so much about so many different things."

"I wonder if there will ever be a man like him again."

The ship was now in. The passengers stood

aside and waited. Then Benjamin Franklin started down the plank!

Again cannons roared! Again bells rang! Again people cheered!

Benjamin Franklin, one of the greatest Americans of all times, was now back in the land he loved so dearly, the United States of America.

Here Benjamin Franklin was to remain until his death on April 17, 1790. He has been honored with all kinds of memorials, statues, and commemorations.

From a simple background Benjamin Franklin became one of the greatest men in history. For his writings, he is called the first truly American author. For his contributions to science he is called a great inventor. For his service to his country during the struggle for independence, he is called a great statesman and patriot. Franklin, himself, merely preferred to be called a printer.